# DELTA FORCE RESCUE

BROTHERHOOD PROTECTORS

*NEW YORK TIMES* BESTSELLING AUTHOR
# ELLE JAMES

EBOOK ISBN: 978-1-62695-275-1

PRINT ISBN: 978-1-62695-276-8

*Dedicated to my editor Delilah Devlin who makes my writing shine. And to my proof readers, Fedora, Sheila, Carmen, Laurel, Rachel and Amanda, who find those pesky typos. And to all my readers who keeping coming back for more. I love writing for you! Thank you for buying my books!*

*Elle James*

# AUTHOR'S NOTE

Visit ellejames.com for titles and release dates
and join Elle James's Newsletter

# CHAPTER 1

BRIANA HAYES HITCHED up her leather satchel, resting the strap on her shoulder as she walked down the stairwell of the rundown apartment building. The day had been long and depressing. She'd already been to six different homes that day. Two of the parents of small children had threatened her. One child had to be removed and placed with a foster family after being burned repeatedly with a cigarette by the mother's live-in boyfriend. Some days, Briana hated her job as a Child Welfare Officer for the state of Illinois. Most days, she realized the importance of her work.

Her focus was the safety of children.

Thankfully, the last home had been one in which the mother seemed to be getting herself together for the love of her child. Because of drug abuse, she'd lost her baby girl to the state. After rehab treatment, she'd gotten a job, proved that she could support herself and the baby and regained custody. Briana prayed the woman didn't fall back into old habits. The child needed a functioning mother to raise her.

The sun had slid down below the tops of the surrounding buildings, casting the streets and alleys into shadow. A chill wind blew dark gray clouds over the sky. The scent of moisture in the air held a promise of rain. Soon.

Briana picked up her pace, hurrying past an alley toward the parking lot where she'd left her small non-descript, four-door sedan. A sobbing sound caught her attention and she slowed. She glanced into the dark alley, a shiver of apprehension running the length of her spine. This part of Chicago wasn't the safest to be in after sunset. Though she didn't want to hang around too long, she couldn't ignore the second sob.

"Hello?" she called out softly.

The sobbing grew more frequent, and a baby's cry added to the distress.

Despite concern for her own safety, Briana stepped into the alley. "Hey, what's wrong? Can I help?"

"No," a woman's voice whispered. "No one can." Though she spoke perfect English, her voice held a hint of a Spanish accent.

Briana squinted, trying to make out shapes in the

shadows. A figure sat hunkered over, back against the wall, holding a small bundle.

"Tell me what's troubling you. Maybe I can help." Briana edged nearer, looking past the hunched figure for a possible trap. When nothing else moved in the darkness, she squatted beside a slight woman, wearing a black sweater and with a hood covering her hair. She looked up at Briana, her eyes red-rimmed, tears making tracks of her mascara on her cheeks.

The baby in her arms whimpered.

"What's your name?" Briana asked.

"I can't." The woman's shoulders slumped.

"My name is Briana," she said. "I just want to know your name."

For a long moment, the young mother hesitated. Then in a whisper, she said, "Alejandra."

"That's a pretty name," Briana said, in the tone she used when she wanted to calm someone who was distraught. "And the baby?"

The woman smiled down at the infant in her arms. "Bella."

"She's beautiful." Briana couldn't leave them alone in the alley. "Do you need help getting home?"

She shook her head. "I can't go there."

"Has someone hurt you?" Briana asked, pulling her phone out of her pocket. "I can call the police. We can have him arrested."

"No!" The woman reached out and grabbed Briana's wrist.

Alarm race through Briana. Instinctively, she drew back.

The woman held tightly to Briana's wrist, balancing the baby in the curve of her other arm. "Don't call. I can't... He can't know where I am."

"If he's threatening you, you need to let the police know," Briana urged, prying the woman's hand free of her wrist. "They can issue a restraining order against him." When the woman shot a glance around Briana, Briana looked back, too. A couple walked past the end of the alley without pausing.

"Are you afraid to go home?" Briana asked.

"I have no home." The mother released Briana's arm and bent over her baby, sobbing. "He had it burned to the ground."

Briana gasped. "Then you *have* to go to the police."

She shook her head. "They can't stop him. He doesn't even live in this country."

"Then how...?"

"He has people," she said. "Everywhere."

Briana sank to her knees beside her. "Why is he doing this to you?"

The woman looked from the baby in her arms up to Briana. "He wants my baby. He won't stop until he has her."

Briana studied the woman and child as the first drops of rain fell. "You can't stay out here. You and the baby need shelter." She reached out her hand. "Come. You can stay at my apartment."

"No." Alejandra shrank against the wall, drawing the baby closer to her. "It's too dangerous for you."

"I'll take my chances," Briana reassured her.

"No. I won't do that to you. He will kill anyone who interferes with his attempt to take my daughter."

"Is he the father?" Briana asked.

Alejandra choked on a sob. "Yes. He is. But he's a very bad man."

"How so?"

"He is *El Chefe Diablo*," Alejandra whispered. "The head of the Tejas Cartel from El Salvador."

Though the word *cartel* sent a shiver of apprehension across Briana's skin, she couldn't ignore the woman and child's immediate needs. "I don't care if he's the head of the CIA or the Russian mafia, you and Bella can't stay out here in the rain. If not for yourself, you need to find real shelter for the baby." Again, she held out her hand. "Come with me. If you won't stay with me, we'll find a safe, anonymous place for you to stay."

Alejandra shook her head. "Anyone who helps me puts themselves in danger."

Briana firmed her jaw. "Again, I'll take my chances. And I know of a place where you won't be found. It's a privately run women's shelter where they don't take names and they don't ask too many questions."

Alejandra looked up, blinking as rain fell into her eyes. "I won't have to tell them who I am?"

"You won't," Briana assured her. She reached out again. "Come on. I'll take you there."

The woman clutched her baby closer. "You... you...aren't working for him, are you?"

"What?" Briana frowned. "No. Of course not. My job is to help children. Your baby needs protection from the rain. *You* need protection from the weather. If you don't come with me, I can't leave you. I'd have to stay here with you." She gave her a twisted smile. "Then we'd all be cold and wet."

"He always finds me. No matter where I go." Alejandra took Briana's hand and let her pull her to her feet. "I can't get away from him."

"We'll get you to the shelter. No one else has to know where you are. Just you, me and baby Bella."

"The people at the shelter?" she asked.

"Won't know who you are. You can tell them your name is Jane Smith."

Her eyebrows rose. "They won't require identification?"

"No. They've even helped immigrants who had nowhere else to turn." Briana slipped an arm around the woman and helped her to her car. "Come on. Get into my car. I can crank up the heater. You two will be warm in no time."

Briana helped Alejandra and the baby into the back seat of the car. "Hold on. I have a blanket I keep in my trunk." She rounded to the rear of the vehicle, popped the trunk lid and reached into the back where she kept a blanket, a teddy bear and bottles of water. She grabbed what she needed and closed the trunk.

Alejandra had buckled herself in and raised her shirt to allow the baby to breast feed.

Briana draped the blanket around the two, handed the woman the plastic bottle of water and laid the teddy bear beside her. "The shelter is about thirty minutes outside of Chicago. You might as well settle in for the ride."

Alejandra nodded and leaned her head back against the headrest. "Thank you." She closed her eyes, her arm firmly tucked around the baby nursing at her breast.

Briana climbed into the driver's seat, shifted into gear and drove out of Chicago to the shelter she knew that didn't require government assistance, therefore wasn't run with all the background checks or identification requirements. Alejandra and Bella would be safe there. Once she had them settled in, she could go home to her apartment, knowing the two were safe from harm and out of the weather, at least for the night.

Traffic was heavy getting out of the city. Eventually, she turned off the main highway onto a secondary highway, and then onto a rural Illinois county road.

A glance in her rearview mirror made Briana smile.

Alejandra, Bella lying in her arms, slept, her tired face at peace except for the frown tugging at her brow.

The wife or girlfriend of the leader of a drug cartel... Briana had run into women who had been on the run from drug dealers, mafia or gang members. Each had been terrified of being found, of their children being taken from them, or murdered. Their fears were founded in truth. Briana had witnessed the aftermath of a gang member's vengeance, and the memory still haunted her. She found it incomprehensible that a man could murder a woman and child out of sheer hatred.

The shelter was located at what had once been a dairy farm. The huge old barn, where the cows had come to be milked, had been cleaned out and converted into living quarters for women and their small children who needed a place to hide away from brutal and abusive relationships. The foundation was funded by a celebrity who preferred to remain anonymous. The rumor had it that the celebrity had once been a woman in need of assistance and a safe house to live in.

Manned by licensed psychologists, social workers and occupational specialists, the shelter was there to provide a place to live and to help the residents learn new skills and, ultimately, become independent and able to take care for themselves. They also had an attorney on retainer to assist the women in getting the restraining orders, separation agreements and divorces they needed in order to start new lives away from toxic situations.

When they arrived at the shelter, Briana parked at the rear entrance, where the people who ran it preferred potential residents to enter. Though they were out in the county, the fewer people who knew of the comings and goings, the better they were able to keep women hidden from their abusive significant others.

As soon as they drove beneath the overhang, a woman emerged from the entrance, a smile and frown of concern on her face. She started to open the passenger seat door but quickly changed to open the back door. "Hello, I'm Sandy. Welcome to Serenity Place."

Briana smiled as she climbed out of the vehicle and stood beside Sandy. "Hi, Sandy. This is…Jane and her daughter, Jill. They need a safe place to stay."

Sandy held out her hand. "You've come to the right place. We're very discreet here. Our primary concern is for the safety of our residents, both big and small."

Alejandra took her hand and let her pull her and the baby out of the car. "Thank you."

In the next few minutes, the woman had Alejandra and Bella assigned to a room with a full-sized bed, a crib and a package of disposable diapers. Once Alejandra had changed Bella's diaper, Sandy took them to a dining room where she helped Alejandra make a sandwich.

"Would you like one, too?" Sandy asked Briana.

She shook her head, though her stomach rumbled. "No, thank you. I need to get back to the city before it gets much later." Briana hugged Alejandra and slipped a business card into her hand. "If you need anything, call me."

The young woman's eyes filled with tears. "You've already done so much."

Briana gave her a gentle smile. "Nothing more than anyone with an ounce of compassion would have done. Take care of yourself and your little one." She brushed a finger beneath the baby's chin then turned to leave.

Sandy followed her to the exit. "We'll take very good care of them."

Briana turned to Sandy. "She's scared. From what she's told me, some very bad people are after her. The baby's father has some connections. If they find her, it won't be good for her or the people harboring her."

"We've dealt with similar situations." Sandy touched her arm. "We'll be on the lookout."

"Thank you, Sandy," Briana said. "You have my number. Call me if you need anything or have any concerns."

She nodded. "Be careful driving back into the

city."

Briana climbed into her car and headed for Chicago. All along the way, she thought about Alejandra and her baby. The desperation in the woman's eyes had struck a chord in Briana's heart. She'd seen that look before in the faces of young mothers she'd visited. Too often, they stayed in bad situations, thinking they had no other alternative. Alejandra had taken the step to get away from the man who'd threatened her and her child. It took a lot of courage to leave an abusive man. The least she deserved was a safe place to hide until she could get back on her feet, maybe change her identity and start a new life somewhere else.

Back at her apartment, Briana climbed the stairs to the second floor and let herself in.

"That you?" her roommate, Sheila Masters, called out from the kitchen.

"It's me," Briana answered as she dropped her keys on the table in the entryway.

"You're late getting home. Did you have a hot date?" Sheila stepped out of the kitchen and handed Briana a glass of wine.

"You're a godsend," Briana said, accepting the offering with a heavy sigh. "I need this and a long soak in a hot tub."

"Go for it. I'll be out here watching some television. I had a busy day at the office. I had to train the new hire." She carried her own wine glass toward the living room, talking as she went. "I don't know why I always get stuck training the new folks."

"Because you have the most patience of anyone in that office. Who else could do it?"

Sheila turned, her lips pinched together. "You're right. Sherry is short-tempered, Lana is too into Lana and Trent is too busy to train anyone himself."

"Which leaves you." Briana touched her friend's arm. "That's why I love you so much. You're the best friend a girl can have. And you have the patience to listen to me vent every day."

"Girl, I don't know how you do it. I'd be a wreck every day." Sheila hugged her. "Go, get that bath. I'll be out here."

Briana nodded, too tired to think beyond the bath and the wine. She took a sip. "I'll be out shortly."

"Take your time. I'll watch the news until you're out."

Once in the bedroom, she dropped her purse on the nightstand, fished out her cellphone and checked for any missed calls. None. Hopefully, Alejandra and Bella were settling into the shelter.

Briana knew she was too sleepy to take a long, hot bath. Instead, she opted for a quick, hot shower, more interested in the wine and propping her feet up than falling asleep in the tub. After her shower, she dried off, stepped into a pair of leggings and was pulling her T-shirt over her head when she heard a loud banging sound from the other room. She'd just stepped out of the bathroom into her bedroom when she heard Sheila scream.

Her heart raced, and her breath hitched in her chest as she ran through her bedroom. She hadn't closed the door all the way earlier. As she reached for the knob, her hand froze.

Through the crack, she saw a man wearing a ski mask, standing over Sheila's crumpled body. He had a gun in his hand with a silencer attached to the end.

Sheila lay motionless on the floor, her eyes open, red liquid pooling beneath her arm.

*Please, let that be wine.*

Briana's gaze went to the coffee table where Sheila's full glass of wine remained unfinished. Her heart sank.

The man nudged Sheila with his boot.

She didn't move, didn't blink her wide-open eyes. Sheila lay still as death.

Briana swallowed hard on a moan rising swiftly up her throat and backed away from the door. Looking toward the window, she shook her head. She'd never get through it without the man hearing her, and the two-story drop could lead to broken bones or death. The bathroom was out of the question. He'd look there next. With nowhere else to go, Briana grabbed her cellphone from the nightstand, dropped to the floor and slid beneath the bed. She dialed 911 and prayed for a quick response, pressing the phone to her ear.

Footsteps sounded, heading into the other bedroom, fading as he moved away.

"You've reached 911. State the nature of your emergency."

"My friend was shot," she whispered.

"Is the shooter still there?" the dispatcher asked.

The footsteps grew louder as they moved toward her bedroom.

"Yes," Briana whispered and gave her address. "Hurry, please." She ended the call, switched the phone to silent and lay still, her gaze on the door as it swung open.

Black boots and black trousers were all Briana could see of the man as he entered the room, stalked to the en suite bathroom and flung open the door.

Briana watched as he disappeared through the doorway. She heard the sound of the shower curtain rings scraping across the metal rod. The boots reappeared, coming to a stop beside her bed. The man's legs bent, and his heels came up as if he was lowering himself into a squat.

Her heart racing, Briana scooted silently across the floor toward the other side of the bed.

The faint sound of a siren wailed in the distance.

The legs straightened, and the boots carried him out of the room. A moment later, silence reigned in Briana's small apartment. She lay for a long moment, counting the seconds since she last heard the sound of footsteps.

The whole time, Briana worried about her friend Sheila. Was she still alive? Had that blood only been a superficial wound? Should she get out from under the bed and find out?

Finally, Briana rolled out from under the bed on the side farthest from the door. She crawled across the carpet and peered through the open doorway into the living room. Sheila lay where Briana had last seen her. Her eyes still open, her face pale, the blood beneath her arm making a dark stain on the white shag area rug they'd purchased together last spring.

Briana glanced toward the entry. The door to their apartment hung open, the doorframe split as if someone had kicked the door in.

Nothing moved. No footsteps sounded on the tile entry.

Still on her hands and knees, Briana crawled toward her friend, tears welling in her eyes, blurring her vision. She had to blink several times to clear them before she could reach for Sheila's neck. Pressing two fingers to the base of her throat, she waited, praying for a miracle.

No pulse. No steady rise and fall of her chest. Nothing.

"Oh, Sheila," Briana whispered, the tears falling in earnest now.

The hole in Sheila's chest told the story.

Briana sat on the floor beside her friend, holding her hand, crying.

Sirens she'd heard moments before now blared loudly outside of the apartment. Soon, several policemen entered, weapons drawn.

Briana looked to them, her heart breaking. "You're too late."

They helped her up and started the interrogation, asking questions she didn't have answers to. Her thoughts went to Alejandra and her baby, but she couldn't say a word about them without giving up their location.

When they were finished, they told her she couldn't remain there. Her apartment was now a crime scene. She would have to find another place to stay. They let her grab her purse and keys but nothing else.

"Do you need someone to drive you to a hotel?" the officer in charge asked.

She shook her head, amazed it didn't fall off as fast as it was spinning. "No," she said. "I can drive myself."

"We can provide an escort, if you'd like," he offered.

"No. I'll be all right," she said, though she knew she was lying.

Walking out of her apartment, she didn't look back. She couldn't. What had happened was inconceivable. Her mind could not comprehend it.

Briana climbed into her car and started the

engine out of sheer muscle memory. When she reached for the shift, her cellphone rang.

She dug in her purse for it and pulled it out, praying it was Sheila claiming it had all been a hoax. *Come back up to the apartment. I'm fine. Everything's fine.*

The phone didn't feel right in her hand, but nothing felt right at that moment. When she swiped her finger across the screen to answer, a voice came across, speaking a language she didn't understand. It took her a moment to realize it was Spanish. "You have the wrong number," she said and started to end the call.

The voice switched to English with a strong Spanish accent. "Who is this? Where is Alejandra?"

Briana pulled the cellphone away from her ear and stared down at it. It had a black case like hers, but the phone wasn't hers. "You will tell me where she is now," the man's voice said. "If you do not, I will find you, and I will make you tell me, if I have to beat the information out of you. Do you hear me?"

"You did this?" Briana asked. "You had my roommate killed in your effort to find Alejandra?"

"I will do whatever it takes to bring her back to El Salvador," the man's voice said.

Anger and raw hatred burned hot inside Briana, bubbling up her throat. "You can rot in hell before I tell you anything." She ended the call, lowered her window and flung the phone out onto the pavement.

"Hell, you hear me?" she yelled. Then she shifted into reverse, backed up a few feet, shifted into drive and ran over the cellphone.

The gesture wouldn't bring back Sheila, but it cut off the man who'd sent his thug to find Alejandra and who had killed her roommate in the process.

As she drove away from her apartment building, Briana knew the man wouldn't stop until he found Alejandra and her child. Briana was the only one who knew who Alejandra was and where she was staying with her daughter, Bella.

If *El Chefe Diablo* was as bad as Alejandra had indicated, he would send his killers after Briana.

She needed help. The police didn't have time to guard her, and they wouldn't do it unless she told them why *El Chefe* was after her. Briana needed someone discreet, someone she could trust implicitly. She pulled out her cellphone and dialed her brother Ryan's number. He was the only man she trusted.

"Hey, Sis," Ryan Hayes answered. "Can't talk long, I'm boarding a plane as we speak and will be out of touch for the next seventeen hours."

A sob escaped her, and she swallowed hard, trying to get words to pass her vocal cords. "Ryan."

"What's wrong," he asked, his words instantly clipped.

She couldn't speak for a full minute.

"Briana? Are you there?" he demanded. "Talk to me. Damned connection."

"I'm here," she said. "I need help."

"Oh, Bree, I'm not even in the States. What's the problem?"

"Sheila's dead," she said, her voice catching. "And I think her killer is coming for me next."

"What the fuck?" Ryan cursed. "I can't be there for another seventeen to twenty hours."

"Don't worry," she said. "I'll figure out something."

"No, wait. I know who you can call until I get back."

"Who?"

"Hank Patterson. Prior Navy SEAL. He has a security service."

"I don't know Hank."

"I have it on really good authority that he's the real deal. He and any one of his guys would lay down their lives for whomever they're protecting. I'll text you the number. Call him. No, never mind. I'll call him and have him contact you."

Briana drove down the street, away from her apartment building, not knowing where she was heading. Headlights in her rearview mirror blinded her until she shifted the mirror. "I don't know where I'll be."

"Don't worry, Bree. Get to somewhere safe. He'll figure it out," her brother said. "And Bree?"

"Yeah," she answered, on the verge of more tears.

"I love you," he said. "Stay safe. You're the only sister I have."

"I love you, too." She ended the call, turned a corner and glanced into the rearview mirror. Were those headlights the same ones that had followed her after leaving her apartment?

Increasing her speed, she rushed to the next corner and turned left, taking the turn as fast as she dared.

Again, the vehicle behind her turned and sped up.

Her heart leaped into her throat. Briana slammed her foot onto the accelerator, shooting her little car forward. She didn't slow when she took the next right turn, the rear end of her car fishtailing around the corner. Punching the gas, she raced to the next intersection where the light had just turned red. Ignoring the light, she shot through right before another car had pulled out.

The driver honked and kept moving forward, blocking the path of the vehicle following her, slowing him enough she was able to speed up and get through the next two lights and turn right then left, zigzagging through the streets until no headlights followed her.

She couldn't stay in Chicago. Briana didn't know where she could stay that would be safe. Going to a friend's house was out of the question. As Alejandra had predicted, being associated with her put others in danger. That was now true for Briana.

Briana had to find a place she could hunker down until help arrived.

# CHAPTER 2

RAFE DONOVAN WAS JUST CLIMBING into his truck after getting fuel at a gas station, when his cellphone vibrated in the cupholder. He noted the name on the screen and answered, "Yo, Hayes, miss me already? I thought you guys were tapped for a mission?"

"We're on our way back. Otherwise, I'd handle this myself," his friend, Ryan Hayes, said. "I just boarded a plane and won't be in contact for at least another seventeen hours, so listen up."

Rafe tensed at the urgency in his friend's voice. "Shoot."

"My sister is in trouble. I spoke with Hank Patterson out in Montana. He says you're the closest asset he has to Chicago, where she lives. He's going to send you to manage this case. You'll get a call from him any minute. I just wanted to give you a heads-up before I go silent in transit."

"What's happening?" Rafe asked.

"I'm not sure, but she needs protection. Her roommate was murdered, and whoever did it is after her now. Where are you?"

"I stopped in Kansas City to visit a buddy of mine on my way out to Montana. I was just about to look for a hotel for the night, but I can be in Chicago in seven hours."

"That's a long time."

Rafe frowned. "It's the best I can do without breaking speed limits."

"I get it," Hayes said. "It would take that long for anyone to fly commercial. My sister's smart enough to find a place to hide out, until then. I'll send her number to you. Expect a call from your new boss as soon as I end this call."

Before Hayes finished talking, another call made Rafe's cellphone vibrate. "I have an incoming call."

"That must be him now," Hayes said. "I gotta go. Take care of my sister. She's the only family I have left. I'm counting on you."

"Will do," Rafe said. "Safe travels, my friend. You're your sister's only blood relative. But you have a shit-ton of brothers who give a damn, too. So, don't fuck up."

Hayes chuckled. "Love you too, bro. Out here."

As soon as Hayes ended the call, Rafe answered the incoming one from Hank Patterson, the owner and founder of the Brotherhood Protectors security agency based out of Eagle Rock, Montana.

"Donovan, here." Rafe started the engine, and the call switched to his truck's speaker.

"You heard?" Hank asked.

"Hayes's sister. Chicago. Yes, sir," he answered, keying Chicago into the map on his cellphone.

"Anything you need, you let me know. If you need a safe house to bring her to, I can't recommend any in Illinois, but I have a couple places here in Montana, if you can get her here."

"Yes, sir. I'll let you know what I find when I get to Chicago." Rafe buckled his seatbelt and pulled out onto the road.

"Anything you require in the way of support, you let me know," Hank said. "Are you armed?"

"Yes, sir." He had a 9mm Glock in the console and an AR15 behind the back seat.

"Good. Let me know when you reach Miss Hayes."

"Yes, sir," Rafe responded. "Out here."

Rafe pulled out of the gas station and onto the interstate highway heading northeast toward Chicago. He could be there by early the next morning, if he didn't run into any construction delays.

A text came through from Hayes with his sister's cellphone number.

Rafe immediately called.

It rang several times before voicemail picked up.

"You've reached the voicemail of Briana Hayes. Please leave a message, and I'll get back to you as soon as possible." Her voice was soft, a little gravely and sexy as hell.

"This is Rafe Donovan, your brother Hayes—" he paused and added, "Ryan, and my boss Hank Patterson said you could use some help. Call me." He ended the call and waited impatiently to hear back from her.

Fifteen minutes passed. Rafe caught himself pushing faster and faster on the interstate and had to slow down to within five miles an hour of the limit. Getting a ticket would be a stupid waste of time, when he needed to get to Chicago as soon as possible. Seven hours stretched in front of him like an interminable amount of time.

Why hadn't she called back? Was she in that much trouble that she couldn't pick up her cellphone and call? Was he too late? Questions rattled around in his mind, and his foot rested heavily on the accelerator. Once again, he had to back off and slow to the limit.

Damn. Why hadn't she called? Twenty minutes passed.

His cellphone chirped through the truck's sound system. Her number appeared on the screen.

Rafe hit the talk button. "Donovan, here."

For a long moment, silence met his greeting. Then that slightly raspy voice sounded through the speakers. "This is Briana."

Rafe let go of the breath he'd been holding. "I've been assigned to protect you, but it'll take me six and a half hours to get to Chicago from Kansas City. Can you wait that long?"

"Guess I'll have to," she said softly. "I'm not in Chicago anymore."

"No? Then, where are you?"

She laughed softly, the sound almost like a sob. "I don't know. Give me a minute. I'll look for a sign."

"You're driving?" he asked.

Again, another sobbing laugh. "I have nowhere else to go. The police kicked me out of my apartment." Her voice hitched. "It's cordoned off as a crime scene." She paused. "Joliet. I'm passing through Joliet."

His chest tightened. The pain in her voice was evident. Apparently, whatever had happened had affected her so much she didn't know where she was going. "What highway?"

"Interstate 80," she said. "I'm coming up to Interstate 55."

"I'm on my way. If you stop, let me know where, and I'll meet you there."

"I'm not stopping. I can't." Another soft sob sounded. "I'm scared."

"Okay. Are you on a handsfree device?"

"If you mean, is my phone connected to my car...it is."

"Good. If you're going to keep driving, take 55

south," he said. "I'm coming across on 72 and will hit 55 in Springfield, Missouri."

When she didn't respond, he prompted, "Can you do that?"

"Yes." Silence stretched between them for several heartbeats. Then she whispered, "Will you stay with me? On the phone?"

"Yes, ma'am," he said, glad she would be in communication all the way. She sounded distraught. If he could keep her talking, he might get her to pull into a hotel and wait for him.

"Just got onto 55," her words came across his speaker.

"Good, just keep going. When you get close to Springfield, Illinois, we'll see how far out I am. We can meet up there or somewhere close to that."

"Okay," she said. "I'm sorry. What did you say your name was?"

"Rafe Donovan."

"Rafe," she said, as if rolling his name across her tongue. He liked the way she said it.

"So, Miss Hayes...do you mind if I call you Briana?" he asked.

"Please. Miss Hayes makes me sound old."

He chuckled. "You don't sound old to me." He'd never been good at chit-chat, but he wanted to hear her voice. It made him feel connected. If she ended the call, he wouldn't know where she was or how she was doing. If she ran off the road, he'd have no idea where to look. "How old are you? Or is that one of those questions a man's not supposed to ask?"

"No. It's okay. I'm twenty-seven," she replied. "How old are you?"

"Old," he said. "I'm thirty-four."

"That's not old."

"Tell that to my body," he said. "It's seen better days."

"How do you know Ryan?" she asked.

"He's one of my teammates." Rafe frowned. "*Was* one of my teammates."

"Was?"

"I separated from the Army a week ago. Your brother and I worked together."

"Delta Force," she stated.

"That's right." He set his cruise control to keep from speeding up and slowing down.

"Ryan and his teammates are pretty tight," Briana said in that soft, gravelly tone.

"It happens when you go through some of the shit we've gone through. Hayes—Ryan—saved my ass on several occasions."

"And I'm sure you returned the favor," Briana said. "My brother calls his teammates his brothers. They're as much a part of his family as I am. Maybe more."

"Don't sell him short. He cares about you. He was on the phone with me right after he hung up with you and Hank. If he hadn't been on a mission, he would've been there for you."

"I know. I hated calling him, but I didn't know what else to do." Her words faded off.

"What happened?" Rafe asked.

"A m-man broke into our ap-partment...and k-killed...my roommate." He could hear the tears in her garbled words.

"Do you need to pull over?" he asked.

For a long moment, she didn't answer.

He worried that she would run off the road because she couldn't see through the tears she must be shedding. "You must have loved your roommate very much," he said in a soothing tone. "What was his name?"

"*Her* name was Sheila," she answered. "He killed Sheila. And yes. I loved her like a sister."

His gut knotted, and his fists tightened around the steering wheel. He'd lost close friends in battle. No amount of words made it better. He didn't begin to think anything he could say to her would make the pain any easier to bear. "I'm sorry."

"She did nothing to deserve what he did to her. Sheila wouldn't hurt anyone."

"Did the homicide detective have any clue as to why he did it?" Rafe asked.

"No. But I think I know why," she whispered.

Not wanting to push her, he waited for her to continue in her own time.

"I helped a woman and her child find shelter. She was running from the child's father. H-he sent the man who broke into our apartment and killed Sheila. He was looking for the woman and the child."

"How do you know this?" Rafe asked.

"I didn't know that I had the woman's cellphone. Her baby's father called it. I answered thinking it was for me. When he didn't get his woman on the line, he demanded I tell him where she was and threatened to come after me." She sniffed. "After what his man did to Sheila…"

"You did the right thing to ask for help."

"I had nowhere else to go. I don't know who works for him or how deep his contacts might be." She drew in a shaky breath. "Someone followed me from my apartment. When I tried to lose him, he remained on my tail, until I ran a stoplight and he was blocked by traffic."

He could hear the terror in her voice. "So, you're the only one who knows where this woman and her child are hidden?"

"The only one who knows who and where she is. The people at the place she's staying don't know her name. I know." She snorted softly. "Sometimes, I wish I didn't. But she's safe for now. I don't know how she lived with the man or how she got away from him with her baby. He's evil. I'm not scared easily, but he has me terrified."

"Hang in there. I'm on my way."

Several minutes passed in silence.

"Still awake?" he asked after a while.

"Barely," she admitted.

"Do you want to pull over at the next hotel?"

"No," she said. "I'm afraid to slow down. He might catch up to me."

"Then talk to me. It might help to keep you awake," he urged.

"About what?"

"Tell me about you," he said. The interstate highway stretched in front of him as he sped across Missouri.

"There's not much to tell."

"From?" he prompted.

"Born in Germany. Dad was in the Army, always deployed. Mom raised us," she said.

"How did you end up in Chicago?"

"My father retired to Bloomington, Illinois. I guess the military was in our blood. As soon as Ryan graduated high school, he joined the Army."

Rafe smiled. "You didn't want to?"

"My father and my mother encouraged me to go to college after Ryan joined the Army. I knew I wanted to work with children, so I studied social work."

"You like children?"

"I do. I wanted a younger brother and sister, but Mom and Dad were happy with just the two of us. We were enough to handle when we had to move so often. I wrote a research paper on causes and the number of cases of child abuse in the state of Illinois. I was appalled by how many were from Chicago and how undermanned the Child Welfare Department was. When I graduated from the university, I applied to the Children and Family Services of Illinois based in Chicago. I've worked there for the past five years, trying to help as many children as I could."

"How's that worked out for you?" he asked.

After a long pause, she said, "I do the best I can to protect children in abusive situations."

"I hear a 'but' in there," he said.

"But sometimes my best isn't good enough to save a child."

"That's got to be tough." He couldn't imagine coming face to face with an adult who repeatedly abused children. He'd put his fist in his or her face for every time they hit, kicked or punched a child.

After a pause, he asked, "Married?"

"No."

"Boyfriend?"

"Once I started work, I never had time. There was always one more child who needed my help." She sighed. "What about you?"

"What about me?"

"Why the Army? Why did you get out?" she asked. "You're not old enough to retire."

He'd agonized over his decision to leave Delta Force. "I didn't come from as stable a family environment as you." He drew in a deep breath and let it out slowly. "My father left when I was only two. My mother raised me alone. No brothers or sisters. She drank. When I was a senior in high school, she got so drunk she wandered outside in the dead of night, in the middle of winter. They didn't find her body until the next morning. She'd passed out in the snow and died where she lay. No one knew. I was asleep in my warm bed." He remembered that morning when the police came to his house, banged on his door and told him his mother had been found.

"You blamed yourself, didn't you?" Briana asked in her soft sexy tone.

Yes, he had. "If I hadn't gone to bed that night, I might have gotten her to put down her whiskey and sleep. She wouldn't have been out wandering around in the freezing temperatures."

"You couldn't have known she would do that," Briana said.

"No, but I should have done more." Rafe had agonized over what he should have done so many times in the years since. Nothing could undo what had happened. His mother was dead. She wouldn't be coming back.

"So, you joined the Army?" Briana spoke softly, reminding Rafe he was in a truck, headed toward a woman he'd never met but spoke so easily with that he felt as if he'd known her for a lifetime.

"I was due to graduate high school at the end of

the month when she died. I was already eighteen, so the child welfare people didn't get all in my face about going to foster care. I ended up staying with a friend until school was out. During that time, I met with a recruiter, signed the papers and waited until I received my high school diploma. Then I shipped out to Basic Combat Training the following week. The rest is history."

"Married?"

"For about a week," he admitted.

She laughed. "I'm sorry. I shouldn't have laughed, but a week?"

He liked the sound of her laughter and wished he could make her laugh more. "We met in Basic Training, married as soon as we graduated and realized it was a mistake when we were shipped to different locations for our advanced training."

"You must have been in love."

"We were in lust or in love with the idea of having someone permanent in our lives." He snorted. "It didn't work for us. We keep in touch through social media and are still friends. She since left the military, married an accountant and has three kids."

"I'm sorry."

"Don't be," he said. "She's happy. I'm happy for her, and her husband seems to be a really nice guy and great father." He shrugged though she couldn't see him. "I realized when I joined Delta Force, I wouldn't have much of a life. I accepted that and swore off long-term relationships. They just don't work."

"They do for some. If you find the right person. I really hope my brother finds the right one for him, someday. He deserves happiness. And he'd make a great father, like our dad."

"You're lucky you had him," Rafe said.

"I know." She sighed. "I wish he would've lived long enough to get to know his grandchildren."

Rafe frowned. "What happened to him?"

"My father took my mother to Chicago for their anniversary. The weather turned cold and icy. They were killed in a twenty-car pileup on the way back. So, you see, Ryan really is all I have left, now that Sheila is gone." Her voice faded out.

"I'm sorry."

"I worry about my brother."

She had every right to worry about him. "I won't lie to you," Rafe said. "Each mission could be his last."

"I know," she said. "But he loves what he does. He feels like he's making a difference."

"Do you?"

"I hope I make a difference in the lives of the children under my supervision," Briana said. "I just wish I could do more to keep them from having to be under my care. So many of their parents didn't have good examples to teach them how to be good parents. A lot of the women had babies in their teens. They were babies themselves."

"You can't save them all," he reminded her.

"I have to remind myself that all the time," she said. "I can't save them all, but if I can save some, it's better than saving none of them."

Once again, silence stretched between them.

"Huh?" her voice came across slightly strained.

"What?"

"I'm just punchy."

Rafe's foot settled on the accelerator, pushing the speed up above the limit by ten miles per hour. "What do you mean? Did something spook you?"

"Yeah, that's it. I'm spooked."

"By what?"

She laughed, the sound tight and unconvincing. "I saw a set of headlights in my rearview mirror."

His hands tightening around the steering wheel, Rafe leaned forward, inching the speedometer up another couple of notches. "Is he catching up?"

"Yes. But I'm sure it's just another motorist trying to get somewhere. There are a few out here. Mostly big rigs."

"Keep an eye on him. When do you stop for gas again?"

"Probably in the next thirty minutes. When I left Chicago, I didn't have a full tank." Her voice crackled.

"Are you hitting a dead zone?" Rafe asked. "You're breaking up."

"Must be. Down...one bar."

"Keep talking," he urged, his chest tight. "You might be able to hear me, even if I can't hear you."

For the next five minutes, he didn't hear anything. He kept talking for the first minute, until his cellphone disengaged from hers. He tried to call her. No answer. Again, he tried.

No answer.

The more time that passed, the more nervous he got. Had she really run into a cellphone dead zone? Or did the headlights following her belong to someone who was after her?

His foot pressed harder on the accelerator. Speed limit be damned. At his best guess, he was still four hours away from her. Not nearly close enough to help if she got in trouble.

Fifteen minutes turned to twenty, and then thirty.

He called repeatedly, praying for an answer, wishing he'd gotten her last location before she'd faded out.

About the time he was ready to give up hope, she answered.

"Briana?"

"It's me," she said, her voice pure music to his ears.

"Thank God."

She laughed. "At first, I realized I was in a short dead zone. Then my battery died on my cellphone, and I didn't have a charger in my car. I had to pull into a truck stop for gas. While I was there, I bought a charging cable."

Rafe eased his foot off the accelerator, dropping from ninety miles per hour to seventy. "Good to hear your voice again. I was worried."

"Sorry. I thought you might be, but I couldn't do anything else."

"Any trouble at the truck stop?" he asked.

"No. I stayed in the well-lit areas, got out to put the pump handle into the car and got back in, locking the door. When it was done, I pulled up to the building before getting out. There were enough people inside to help, if I needed it. Anyway, I'm back on the road and should be in Springfield in an hour and a half."

"I should be there about the same time, maybe a little later."

"I'll continue through to find Interstate 72 and meet you on your side when you get there."

"Sounds like a good plan," he said.

"It's good to hear your voice," she said. "I know it's silly, but I feel safer when I'm talking with you."

"And I feel better about you when I can hear you."

She laughed. "It's strange, isn't it? I feel like I know you already. Like we've known each other for a long time."

"We have. For at least a couple hours," he said, smiling.

"How often do people really take the time to listen to each other? We're all so busy with our own lives, we don't have time to really get to know each other."

Rafe chuckled. "And here we are...strangers... getting to know each other."

"Thanks for taking the time to talk to me when you really didn't have to," she said. "Or is this part of your job, to protect me by keeping in touch?"

"Does it matter?" he asked. "For the record, I'm glad we're talking. It'll make it easier when we meet in person."

"None of that awkward getting-to-know-you stuff, right?" she said. "Tell me a little more about you."

"You know my life history. What more is there?"

"A lot. Like, do you prefer mountains or beaches? What's your favorite color? Dogs or cats?"

"You first," he countered. "Mountains or beaches?"

"Mountains," she said. "I like beaches, but there's something so serene and peaceful about the mountains. I always dreamed of going back to the Rockies. We vacationed there as a family when I was a teen. Now, you."

"Mountains. You can get lost in the mountains and find yourself there. I did that once. Spring break one year, I drove out to Colorado with a friend. We hiked so many trails and never saw another soul. The air was so crisp and clean, unlike the pollution and light noise of Minneapolis where I lived with my mother."

"Minneapolis, huh? And you're going to work for Hank Patterson? He's based out of Montana, from what my brother told me. He's told me he wants to work for Hank when he leaves the military."

"It's a good choice, from what I hear from other men I know who've gone to work there. He hires former Special Forces soldiers, SEALs and marines. Gives them work that suits the skills they learned on active duty."

"Sounds like a good gig," she said.

"I'll let you know after my first assignment," he said, his lips quirking upward.

"Me." She sighed, the sigh sounding more like a yawn at the end.

"Are you getting sleepy?" he asked. "You can pull over. I'll get there as soon as I can."

"No. I don't want to stop. I can stay awake, if we keep talking. My favorite color is blue. The blue of the sky after a summer rain. And though I like all cats and dogs, I prefer dogs, though it's been a long time since I've had one. And they like me for whatever reason. What about you?"

He smiled at her words. "I like blue for the same reason. The blue of the skies I saw in Colorado make me want to head back to the mountains."

"Cats or dogs?"

"I had a cat and a dog growing up. I like the independence of cats but prefer the pure affection and loyalty of a dog."

They talked for the next hour, learning more about the places they'd been—Briana as a military brat, Rafe during his assignments with the military. They shared items on their bucket lists. They both wanted to see Devil's Tower Monument, the Tetons and Yellowstone.

As they neared Springfield, Rafe could tell Briana was getting sleepier. He looked at the hotels on the east side of the city then, put Briana on hold for a few minutes, called ahead and reserved a room with two beds. When he got there, he'd insist on them sleeping for a few hours before they decided where to go next.

"I've sent you a map pin of the place we'll meet. You should be there in twenty minutes. I'll be there about the same time, give or take a few minutes. Wait for me there. Stay in your car until I arrive. I'm in a black four-wheel-drive pickup."

"I'm in a small, silver four-door Nissan," she said. "I'm looking forward to meeting you in person."

"Me, too." He said and meant it. "None of the awkward stranger greetings."

"That's right," she said. "We're practically old friends."

"That's right," he said.

"Old friends meeting at a hotel." She laughed. "That's not awkward at all. If I wasn't so tired, I might think it strange and a little weird."

"But not awkward," he finished.

"Right," she said. "I'm pulling off the interstate now."

"Me, too." Rafe exited the interstate. He could see the hotel sign clearly. His pulse quickened. After being on the phone for hours with Briana, he'd finally get to meet her. No, he didn't feel awkward. Yes, he was excited.

# CHAPTER 3

BRIANA PARKED beneath the overhang at the entrance to the hotel and waited inside her car. Headlights flashed behind her. When she glanced in the rearview mirror, her heart fluttered. The big shiny grill of a pickup came to a stop behind her. A door opened, and a tall, muscular man wearing jeans and a black T-shirt climbed out.

All the time she'd spent on the phone with Rafe Donovan, she'd had an image in her mind of what he'd look like.

Her heart beat faster as he stepped into the light and walked up to the driver's side window.

Rafe Donovan was all she'd imagined and so very much more. Yes, he was tall, broad-shouldered and built like a brick wall. In addition, the man was hot enough to melt her bones.

If she hadn't been so distraught by all that had

happened, she would have groaned at her own appearance, meeting the man for the first time in person. But her looks meant nothing in light of having lost her best friend.

Briana was just glad Rafe was there. Already, she felt better and more secure. She unlocked her door.

He opened it and held out his hand. "Briana?" he asked.

She nodded and laid her hand on his. "You don't even know how glad I am to finally see you."

He helped her out of the vehicle.

Her legs shook, and she would have fallen, but he wrapped his arm around her middle.

"I know you've been through a lot, but let's get inside and into a room before we relax," he said with a crooked smile.

She nodded, holding back ready tears. She swallowed hard on the lump blocking her throat and let him guide her into the building to the front desk.

"I have a reservation for Rafe Donovan," he said.

The clerk had him sign a card, handed him a key and pointed to the elevator. "Check out is at ten, but since you two are arriving so late, I'll make a note to hold the cleaning until one."

"Thank you," Rafe said. "I'll be back in a few minutes to move the vehicles."

With his arm around her, Rafe led her to the elevator and up to the third floor.

She walked in a daze, leaning into his solid form, glad for his strength and presence. She wasn't alone.

Once they were inside the room, he nodded toward the two beds. "I know we just met, but I can't keep an eye on you if you're in a different room. I promise to keep my hands to myself."

She stared at the two beds then turned her gaze to him. "Thank you. I'm just glad you're here." She bit her bottom lip to keep it from trembling. She could feel the waterworks welling in her eyes. The dam that had held back the tears was crumbling quickly.

"Come here," he said, opening his arms.

Briana fell into him and buried her face against his chest. The emotions she'd kept at bay throughout the long drive refused to be contained a moment longer. Tears streamed down her face and soaked his dark T-shirt. "I'm sorry. I just can't stop."

"It's okay. You've been through a lot."

For a long time, she stood in his arms, letting the tears fall.

Rafe held her throughout, smoothing a hand over her hair, murmuring soothing words Briana couldn't make sense of.

"I can't…" she whispered, "…can't get Sheila's face out of my mind. She was staring at me, and she was…dead."

"Not long ago, I held one of my best friends in my arms as he'd bled out in the back of a helicopter. His name was Freestone. Justin Freestone. He looked up

44

at me, square in the eye, and asked, "Am I going to die?"

Briana stilled, Rafe's words cutting through her own grief. She could hear the torture in his own tone. She raised her face and looked into shadowed eyes. "Did you know?"

Rafe nodded. "He'd taken a hit so bad, he wasn't going to make it back to base."

"What did you say?"

His lips twisted. "No, buddy. We're going to get you a first-class ticket home to your wife and family. Hang in there. Freestone, you're going home."

"I'm so sorry." She pressed her palm against his cheek and leaned up on her toes, brushing her lips across his.

Rafe's arm tightened around Briana. He stroked her hair, cupped the back of her head and lowered his mouth to hers. His lips hovered over hers.

"I didn't get to say goodbye," she said.

"I know. Shhh," he said, his breath mingling with hers. "You're tired. You need sleep."

"I am," she said. "But I need this more." She leaned up on her toes, just enough to press her mouth to his.

What started as her move changed halfway through the kiss. He pulled her closer, until their bodies were flush up against each other and his hand swept up beneath her hair.

His mouth claimed hers in a kiss that pushed all other thoughts from her mind. All she could feel, think, hear or see was this man who'd spent the last few hours getting to know her over the phone.

Never had she felt so safe, so warm and protected. As the kiss continued, her feelings changed from safety to longing to need. She needed to be closer. The kind of closer that included skin to skin contact.

Briana slid her hands up his chest and locked them behind the back of his neck. She didn't need to breathe when she had him. She could die in his arms and have no regrets.

Alas, Rafe lifted his head and brushed back a strand of her hair from her forehead. "You need rest. We have to make some decisions in the morning about what's next, but for now…sleep."

He was right. She'd had a long day, and it was already three in the morning. The next day didn't promise to be any shorter. If she wanted to have functioning brain cells to solve the problems of her current situation, she needed rest.

"I don't have any clothes," she said.

"I do. You can borrow shorts and a T-shirt to sleep in. I'll go get them out of my truck and move the vehicles to a parking space."

When he turned to leave, her heart leaped up her throat, and she grabbed his arm. "You're coming back, right?"

He smiled and cupped her cheek. "I won't be gone but a couple minutes. Lock the door with all the locks after I leave, and don't open the door for anyone but me."

Briana nodded. Her pulse pounded so loudly against her eardrums she could barely hear herself think. "I will." She let go of his arm and stepped backward, her hands clutched in front of her. Now that she was with him, she didn't want him out of her sight. But that was silly. What could go wrong in a few short minutes?

"You can shower while I'm downstairs."

Her heart hammered against her ribs. The last time she'd showered, she'd only been in the bathroom a few minutes. Long enough for someone to break into her apartment, kill her roommate and change her life forever. She shook her head. "I'll wait until you get back."

He nodded and turned toward the door. He checked through the peep hole before opening it. "Lock up behind me," he said as he left the room.

Briana twisted the bolt on the door and threw over the metal latch. When she checked through the peephole, Rafe still stood outside the door.

"Did you turn the lock?" his muffled voice sounded through the thick door.

"Yes," she answered.

"I'll be right back." And he left the door, walking toward the stairwell.

Briana stood at the door for the next minute,

staring out at the empty hallway. The other guests would be sound asleep.

Not Briana. Her body was tense, her pulse jumping, her breath caught and held in her lungs until she had to draw more in.

What was probably only five minutes felt like hours.

Briana knew staring through the peephole wouldn't make the time pass any faster. She stepped away and paced across the room. At every sound, she hurried back to the door to look out through the tiny hole.

When at last a soft knock sounded at the door, she raced to answer, looking first through the peephole to verify it was Rafe.

She quickly unlocked the door and jerked it open.

He stepped in, dropped a duffle bag on the floor and turned to lock the door behind him.

When he faced her again, she threw herself into his arms.

"Hey." He chuckled. "I was only gone five minutes, tops."

"I know. But if felt like forever." She clung to him for another moment before loosening her hold around his neck.

His hands gripped her around the waist. "Not that I mind a beautiful woman throwing herself at me. It's kind of nice. You know…helps the old ego."

"You're not old," she said, her cheeks heating. "I'm

just…grateful." And a whole lot more emotions she wouldn't care to admit to a man she'd just met.

He lifted the duffle bag and carried it to the bed where he unzipped it and pulled out a T-shirt and a pair of gym shorts. "Sorry, but this is about the extent of my wardrobe. No robe. But I do have a comb, and I brought a spare toothbrush from the front desk." He handed her a comb, toothbrush and a travel-size tube of toothpaste.

"It's all perfect," she said. Gathering the items, she entered the bathroom and stared at the shower. Her body started trembling.

"What's wrong?" he asked, coming up behind her.

"N-nothing."

"Remember? We're old friends," Rafe slipped his arms around her from behind and crossed them over her belly. "You can tell me anything," he said, his warm breath stirring the hair beside her ear.

"I had just gotten out of the shower and dressed when the man broke into our apartment."

His arms tightened briefly. Then he let go, moved around her, swept back the curtain, switched on the water and stood back. "Get in. When you're ready, let me know. I'll open the door a crack and talk to you the whole time, if you like."

She thought about it for a moment, and then nodded. "It's silly to be afraid."

"No, it's not." He smoothed a strand of her hair back from her forehead, tucked it behind her ear, and then rested his palm against her cheek. "You had something terrible happen to a good friend of yours in your own home. You *should* be afraid. And if it helps to leave the door open, we'll leave the door open. I'm here. I'm not going to let anything happen to you."

She captured his hand and turned it over, pressing her lips against his lifeline. He was her lifeline. "Thank you." Briana entered the bathroom, closed the door and leaned her ear against it.

"I'm still here," he said through the door.

She smiled, quickly stripped out of her shoes, leggings, T-shirt, bra and panties. After adjusting the temperature of the water, she stepped behind the curtain. "Okay," she called out.

A draft of cool air ruffled the shower curtain.

"I'm right outside the door if you want to talk," he said. "You can pretend you're still in your car, which is now parked outside beneath a bright light."

"Thank you for moving it," she said. "And thank you for being patient with me." She squirted some of the hotel-supplied shampoo into her palm, wet her hair and rubbed the soap into it, trying to come up with a topic to talk about. It felt as if they'd talked about so much already. "What kind of music do you like to listen to?"

"I like country and jazz, but I'm a big fan of rock and roll. What about you?" His voice sounded close, as if he were standing in the bathroom beside the shower.

Briana peeked around the side of the curtain, suds slipping down her cheek.

Rafe leaned his back against the doorframe, facing into the bedroom, his arms crossed over his chest. He wasn't looking her direction. Instead, he was giving her the privacy she needed, while providing the comfort of knowing he was nearby. A gentleman. Who knew they still existed?

She ducked behind the curtain and tipped back her head beneath the water. "Rock and roll, pop and country. I do like jazz and R&B, as well."

"What about books?" he asked. "Fiction? Non-fiction?"

"Fiction. I like to escape when I read," she said. "You?

"Non-fiction. I studied a lot of history and biographies. I'm interested in how people lived through the centuries. I also like books on how things work."

Briana squeezed conditioner into her palm and worked it into her hair. With only a comb to work with, she'd have to be careful not to get too many tangles. When they left the hotel, she'd ask Rafe to stop at a store so that she could buy a few necessities, like a brush, underwear, another shirt and, maybe, a pair of jeans. She wasn't sure how long it would be before she got back to Chicago, and if the police would allow her back into her apartment anytime soon. "I'll need to call my boss and let her know I won't be in for a few days."

"We'll need to talk about where we're going from here."

The thought of making a decision left her cringing in the shower. "Could we do that after we sleep?"

"Absolutely," he replied.

She washed her body with soap, her thoughts going to Rafe's strong arms and big hands. A shiver of awareness ran over her. The man was steps away from her naked body. If she knew him better...if they were dating...she'd invite him in to share the shower with her.

Heat built inside, pooling at her core, followed quickly by guilt. Her friend had died, and she was thinking of getting naked with a stranger.

But she and Rafe weren't strangers. They were practically old friends.

All the more reason for her to stop thinking about showering with the man.

After rinsing thoroughly, she switched off the water. "I'm done."

"I'll just close the door." His deep voice filled the bathroom.

She waited to hear the soft snick of the door closing before she pulled back the curtain and stepped out onto the mat.

Minutes later, she'd dried, pulled his large T-shirt over her head and let it fall down around her thighs. The shorts were too long, covering her knees, and she had to roll the waistband a few times to keep them from falling off her hips. She rinsed her panties in the sink and hung them to dry on one of the towel racks. Then she plugged in the blow dryer and worked the tangles out of her hair with the comb, blowing it dry at the same time. Satisfied she was clean of the smell of fear and death, she stepped out of the bathroom wearing Rafe's T-shirt and shorts.

He lounged on one of the beds with his hands laced behind his head. He smiled when he saw her. "That T-shirt looks better on you than me." His brow wrinkled as his gaze shifted lower. "The shorts, not so much."

"Thanks for the loan. I'm just glad to have something to wear." She padded across room and stared at the other bed.

"You can have this one," he offered. "I thought you'd want me to be closer to the door."

"This one is fine," she said, but she couldn't force herself to get under the covers. Images of her apartment, Sheila's lifeless body lying on the floor, and the EMTs loading her onto a stretcher all flooded back to her.

Rafe's hands settled on her shoulders.

Briana hadn't even heard him get out of the bed to come stand behind her.

"What's wrong?"

"How do you turn off the images? My mind is like a movie film on an infinite loop. It keeps replaying the man in my apartment, him standing over Sheila and then searching the rest of my place. I see him standing beside the bed I hid beneath."

Rafe eased her back against him. "You need to sleep."

"How?" She shook her head. "How do I turn it off?"

"I can't tell you that. I've never been able to do that myself. Especially right after the event happened. At the very least, you need to lie down and rest."

She looked over her shoulder into his face. "I'm afraid to close my eyes."

"Then lie on the bed and keep your eyes open. Relaxing has to be of some help. And maybe, you'll fall asleep."

She nodded and took a step toward the bed and stopped. "I'm afraid."

"Get in and scoot over. I'll hold you until you go to sleep." He pulled back the comforter and waved her toward the bed.

Briana slipped between the sheets and moved over to allow him to slide in beside her.

He'd kicked off his boots and changed into shorts while she'd been in the shower. He smelled faintly of a musky aftershave, and his body was warm and reassuringly solid beside her.

Once he was settled in the bed, she rolled into his side and rested her head on his shoulder. "Do you mind?"

He hesitated. "No. But don't be alarmed if I like this too much. It's been a while since I've been with a woman."

"I'm sorry." She leaned away from him. "Am I bothering you?"

He chuckled. "Only in the best way," he said. "Lie still and stare at the ceiling. It's boring enough to put you to sleep. Light on or off?"

"On, please."

"On, it is." He pulled her close, his arm around her shoulder, his hand resting on her side. "Rest, Briana. We'll tackle the world when we wake."

For the longest time, she lay awake in Rafe's arms, staring at that boring ceiling. Rafe was right. She stared at it long enough it lulled her into a dreamless sleep. Briana woke several hours later spooned into the curve of Rafe's body. The sun had yet to rise, but the gray light of pre-dawn crept into the room around the edges of the blackout curtains.

She lay there, listening to the sound of Rafe's breathing. He'd been patient with her when she'd been scared, and he'd talked to her for the hours it took for them to finally meet in person. He hadn't had to do all that. She was an assignment to him. But he was going above and beyond what she would expect of a bodyguard.

She pressed her back into his front, laid her head on his thickly muscled arm and allowed herself to close her eyes. The disturbing images remained floating in the back of her mind but pushed way back. At that moment, Rafe's presence dwarfed any other thoughts, and soon, she fell asleep and slept through the remainder of the night without dreams. When she woke, light streamed through the window, and she was alone in the bed.

Briana sat up straight, her heart pounding. "Rafe?"

# CHAPTER 4

WHEN HE HEARD Briana's cry, Rafe stepped out of the bathroom, barefooted, rubbing a towel over his wet hair.

She was finally awake, but the fear in her eyes tugged at his heart.

"Hey," he said with a smile, hoping to calm her. "Glad you finally decided to wake up. We're due to check out in thirty minutes. You all right? Or do I need to ask them to put us up for another night?"

"No. I'm awake. I can be ready by then." She blinked, the fear fading from her face, though the shadows remained. Flinging aside the comforter, she swung her legs over the side of the bed and stood, staring at him, her shoulders slumped. "I was hoping I'd wake in my own bed and everything that happened yesterday was all part of a horrible nightmare." Tears welled in her eyes. "She's gone, though, isn't she?"

Rafe's heart squeezed hard in his chest. He didn't have words that could help her through the pain. Instead, he opened his arms.

Briana walked into them. "I know crying doesn't help." She sniffed, drew in a deep breath and wrapped her arms around his waist, resting her cheek against his chest. "I promise I'll pull myself together. Soon."

"You're allowed to grieve," he said. "You wouldn't be human if you didn't."

For a long moment, she remained in his arms, her body warm from the bed, her hair smelling of the shampoo she'd used the night before.

Rafe could have stood there forever. Briana, the stranger who wasn't such a stranger, fit perfectly in his arms and felt so right.

She lifted her head and stepped back. "Thank you for your patience." Her shoulders squared, and her jaw firmed. "I'll be ready in five minutes."

"You have thirty," he reminded her.

"I need to call my boss and let her know what's going on. I should have done it hours ago." She reached for her cellphone, hit her boss's number and waited.

Rafe studied her as she told her boss she wouldn't be in and why. His heart hurt for her as she spoke of the murder. When tears slipped down her cheeks, she wiped them away with the back of her hand. "I need the next few days off. No, I don't know how long. For now, consider me off for the next two weeks. I'll let you know if I'm coming back sooner." She ended the call, wiped her wet cheeks and pasted a weak smile on her face. "Now that that's over, I'll just duck into the bathroom. I won't be long."

His brow furrowed as he looked down at her. "Are you sure you're okay?"

She nodded. "I might not be now, but I will be. I want to call the shelter where the woman and her baby are hiding, but I'm afraid any contact with them will only lead others to them."

"I might be able to help. My boss, Hank Patterson, has a team of people with various skills. One of them is supposedly good at anything to do with computers and communications equipment. We could have him contact the people at the facility. That way, if your phone is being tracked, the call wouldn't be coming from you."

She nodded. "That makes sense. And I really need to know they're okay." Briana grabbed her clothes and shoes and entered the bathroom, pausing at the door. "You'll be here when I get out?"

He raised both hands. "I promise. I'm not going anywhere without you."

She nodded and closed the door.

As promised, she was out a few minutes later, her hair neatly combed, wearing her own T-shirt and leggings. The shirt and shorts she'd slept in were neatly folded in her hands.

He took them from her and packed them in his duffle bag. "Might need these again. I'm not sure where we're going from here."

"Maybe we should go back to Chicago. At least, there, I might be able to get into my apartment for some of my own things."

"That's a possibility, but I'm not convinced it's safe."

"Whoever is after me wouldn't know your truck. I could drive my car to the edge of the city and park it in a commuter lot," Briana suggested.

"We could do that," he said. "I'd like to get my boss's take on it first."

"Okay." Her stomach rumbled, and she grimaced. "I need to eat something. I haven't had anything since lunch yesterday."

"Then let's go find food. While we're eating, we can discuss where to go from here." He slung the duffle bag over his shoulder, checked the hallway through the peephole and opened the door. The corridor was empty except for the rolling cart filled with clean linens, towels and toiletries.

"Come on," he said, waving her through, his hand on the strap of his backpack, the other on the gun in the holster beneath his jacket.

He hadn't worn it into the hotel the night before but had brought it inside hidden in his duffle bag. His gut told him things could be different today, and he needed to be prepared for anything.

When Briana turned toward the elevator, Rafe blocked her path. "Let's take the stairwell. It's only two flights, and we control when the door opens."

Her brow puckered. "You think we're in danger here?"

"I'd rather not take any chances on my first assignment." He winked, and then his jaw hardened. "Seriously, until we know what we're up against, we can't take anything for granted."

She nodded. "I'm leaving it up to you."

He led the way to the stairwell, descending at a pace she could easily keep up with. When they arrived at the ground floor, he went through first and out into the parking lot, checking all directions before he went back to get her and led her out to his truck, using his body as a shield for hers.

He'd opened the passenger side door and was waiting for Briana to climb in, when she glanced around him and her eyes widened. "Sweet Jesus!"

"What?" He spun to see what she was talking about.

A black and white border collie ducked between vehicles parked in the lot. A car leaving nearly hit the animal and honked.

Briana flinched and started around Rafe. "He's going to get hit."

He gripped her arm, holding her back. "Forget the dog. You need to get into the truck."

She tugged at the hand restraining her. "We can't leave the dog. He could wander out onto the highway and get hit."

"If you don't get into the truck, you could be targeted by the people who killed your friend." He urged her toward the open door of his truck.

Her eyebrows lowered. "I will, but we need to do something about that dog."

Rafe sighed. "Will you at least stand behind the door for protection, while I go after the dog?"

She nodded. "I'll stay. Just grab him before it's too late."

Rafe was torn between going after the dog and staying at Briana's side. If he didn't save the dog, the woman would do it herself. Either way, she would be exposed.

He pointed to her. "Stay." Then he walked toward the dog. "Hey, big guy," he spoke softly, holding his hand out to the border collie.

The dog edged toward him, his nose out, sniffing. He whined and wagged his tail. Before he reached Rafe, the dog dropped to the ground, his entire back end wagging along with his tail.

As Rafe dropped to his haunches, the crack of gunfire sounded. Something whizzed over the top of his head and hit the stone façade of the hotel, kicking out fragments of rock.

Rafe dropped to the ground, shouting over his shoulder. "Briana, get down!" He low-crawled on his elbows and knees toward the closest vehicle.

The dog dove beneath the chassis.

Rafe came up on his haunches between two cars and glanced toward Briana.

She'd dropped to the ground and scooted beneath the truck, her head up, eyes rounded.

Rafe pointed toward her and mouthed the word "stay".

Briana nodded and scooted even further beneath the truck chassis, hiding behind one of the wheels.

Rafe gauged the trajectory of the bullet, turned and edged toward the back of the vehicles. A dark SUV parked on the other side of the street pulled away from the curb, made a U-turn in the middle of the road and barreled into the hotel parking lot, heading directly for Rafe's pickup and Briana.

Hunkering low, Rafe ran behind the backs of the vehicles toward Briana, pulling his gun out of the holster beneath his jacket.

The passenger door of the SUV opened. A man dressed in black clothes and a black ski mask started to get out.

Rafe's heart leaped. He leaned over the hood of a vehicle, sighted his weapon on the man and pulled the trigger.

The window beside the man exploded in little

shards of glass. The man jumped back into the vehicle, and the SUV raced directly for Rafe.

Rafe dove away from the car he'd leaned on and rolled out of the path of the speeding vehicle.

The SUV plowed into the spot where Rafe had been standing, pushing the car into the one next to it. The barrel of a military-grade rifle poked through the shattered window, aiming toward Rafe where he lay on the ground.

He rolled beneath a minivan and out the other side as bullets pelted the ground he'd been lying against a moment before.

Leaping to his feet, Rafe aimed and fired at the passenger door where the rifle poked through. The rifle clattered against the glass and disappeared inside. The SUV's driver backed out of the mangled car, shifted into drive and raced out of the hotel parking lot.

Rafe remained where he was, a minivan hood between him and the disappearing SUV. When the SUV was out of rifle range, Rafe ran to his truck and held out his hand. "Come on, we need to leave before he decides to return and finish one or both of us off."

Briana crawled out from beneath the truck and took his hand.

Rafe pulled her to her feet and into his arms, crushing her to his chest. Her body trembled against his. "You're shaking."

"Give me a break. It's not every day my friend is murdered, and my bodyguard is shot at."

He tipped her head up, kissed her hard and lifted her up into the seat. "Stay low as we drive out of here."

She nodded and buckled her seatbelt.

Before he could close the door, a black and white streak of hair dashed between him and the door. The dog he'd leaned down to pet leaped into the truck and settled on the floor at Briana's feet.

Rafe started to tell the animal to get out.

Briana, hunching over in the front seat, ruffled the hair around the dog's neck. "Let him stay. He has a collar with a tag on it. We can call the owner after we get out of here."

He ran around to the driver's side, jumped in, revved the engine and took off in the opposite direction from their attackers.

As they pulled away from the hotel, Briana, lying on her side on the console, keyed the phone number from the tag on the dog's collar.

"Hello, this is Briana. We found your dog in a hotel parking lot." She listened, her brow knitting. "Yes, that's the hotel... There is?" Her frown deepened. "I'm so sorry to hear that." Her gaze went to the border collie. "How do you want us to get the dog to you? We're kind of in a hurry to get back on the road."

Rafe leaned closer to her, trying to watch the road

and eavesdrop on the conversation. He couldn't hear what the dog's owner was saying.

"Are you sure? I mean, she's beautiful and obviously well taken care of. Okay. We'll make sure she goes to a good home. Thank you and my condolences." Briana ended the call. "Is it safe for me to sit up? I'm getting a crick in my neck."

Rafe had been watching as he drove toward the interstate. "Yes, if you keep fairly low."

She sat up, sliding low in her seat. "Apparently, we've just adopted a dog."

"What?" He shot a glance her way.

"The man I talked to just lost his father. His father's border collie, Lucy's her name, keeps escaping the son's backyard and coming to the cemetery behind the hotel to visit his former owner." Briana leaned forward, smoothing her hand over the collie's head. "She misses him. The man's son has children, a full-time job and his wife works. They don't have time to keep chasing down Lucy and bringing her home. And they're afraid she'll get run over, which would have broken his father's heart."

"What are we going to do with a dog?" Rafe asked, thinking of the complications a dog could add to the job of keeping Briana safe.

"I guess we'll need to stop for a few essentials, like a leash, bowls, food, water and toys." Her lips twitched at the corners. "And don't even think we'll drop her off at the nearest shelter. She's been through so much already."

"You're running from a killer. We can't afford the distraction." Rafe frowned at Lucy. "No offense."

"Yeah. I get that," Briana said. "I also know that we aren't leaving her in that hotel parking lot. It was only a matter of time before she was hit by a vehicle."

Rafe wasn't going to talk Briana out of keeping the dog. He sighed and cast a worried glance at the border collie. "Give us any trouble and your ass is getting booted out of this truck." He pointed his finger at the dog. "Got it?"

Lucy barked and licked his pointed finger.

Briana laughed. "I think she gets it."

"Border collies are one of the most intelligent breeds of dogs." Rafe's brow dipped as he changed the subject. "What worries me is how those guys found you."

"Couldn't they have followed me from Chicago?"

"Maybe, but I doubt it. I'm betting they've tapped into the GPS on your cellphone. They followed you to your apartment because you had the woman's cellphone. They figured out who you are once they realized they murdered your roommate." He held out his hand. "Give me your cellphone."

She frowned. "You think they followed my cellphone? How?"

"Hacking into phone records."

"So quickly?"

He nodded. "They probably have connections with hackers on the dark web." He wiggled his fingers. "Your phone."

She laid her cellphone in his palm.

Rafe turned the truck into a gas station, rolled down the window and started to toss the phone into the trash.

Briana grabbed his arm before he could throw it and pointed to a truck full of furniture and household items with a sign painted on the side that said GEORGIA OR BUST. She smiled, took the phone from Rafe, lowered her window and dropped the phone into the bed of the pickup.

Rafe chuckled as he left the station and drove up the ramp onto the interstate headed west. His gaze took in every direction, searching for the dark SUV with the busted window.

"Have we decided where we're going?" Briana asked.

"I figure our current location has been compromised." Rafe's jaw tightened. "We need to get somewhere safer than the interstate. Safer than Illinois."

Briana looked to him. "You have a place in mind?"

"I didn't. But Hank Patterson sent me the location of a place that will work for us. We just have to get to Montana."

Her eyes widened. "We're going to Montana?"

He nodded, the idea resting well with him. He didn't know what they'd do once they reached the hunting cabin in Eagle Rock, but Hank had assured him the cabin was remote, hard to find and he'd have the guidance and help he'd need to keep Briana safe.

"You might as well settle back." He set the cruise control for five miles per hour over the posted limit. "It's a long way."

"How long?" she asked, her gaze seeking his.

"About twenty hours."

"Wow, that is a long way from home." She stared out the front windshield at the road ahead, the corners of her mouth turning downward. "But then, what home do I have? I can't go back to my apartment. I need clothes, but I can buy those. I have no family in Illinois." She gulped back what sounded like a sob. "My boss doesn't expect me back anytime in the next couple of weeks." Briana shrugged. "Might as well go to Montana." She gave him a weak smile, her hand buried in Lucy's fur. "Hear that, Lucy? We're going to Montana. I just hope the guys who attacked us don't decide to follow."

Rafe felt the same way. He could be taking the problem with them. At least, in Montana, he'd have backup.

# CHAPTER 5

NUMEROUS TIMES during the long journey, Briana asked Rafe to let her drive to give him a break. He'd refused, stating he was used to being up for long hours and didn't fall asleep in vehicles.

He might not sleep in vehicles, but once the sun set, *she* did, and she slept hard until morning light. She yawned and stretched, amused to find Lucy lying half on the floor, half across her lap, the dog's head resting in her palm.

Briana smiled softly down at the dog who had been grieving for her former owner. "Poor baby. You miss your guy. I miss my friend. We're a pretty sad pair." She glanced up, blinking back some pesky tears. "Where are we?"

Rafe drew in a deep breath and let it out. "Montana. We're about an hour and a half from Eagle Rock."

"Is Hank expecting us? I thought I heard you talking on the phone a little while ago."

He nodded. "About an hour ago, I called Hank to let him know we were on our way in. He said we could crash there for a day if we wanted, until we can get a better handle on who is after you and how to stop them. However, I think it would be better if we go straight to the hunting cabin he has lined up for us. I don't want to put Hank and his family at risk by our staying with them."

"Agreed," she said. She wished she'd known Alejandra's phone had been in her purse when she'd entered her apartment. Had she known, Sheila might not be dead. Then again, she'd had no idea how far *El Chefe* would go to find his woman and child.

"We'll need to give Hank more information about this guy who's threatening you, so that his computer guru, Swede, can run some checks, maybe find out who he's hired to do his dirty work. Also, so that he can check on the woman and her baby."

"I can tell you the name of the man she said is after her and the baby. He's from El Salvador. His name is *El Chefe Diablo.*"

Rafe's head jerked around, and the truck slowed. "Who did you say?"

"*El Chefe Diablo* from El Salvador. Apparently, he's a very dangerous man."

"You've never heard of him before now?" Rafe asked.

Briana shook her head. "I've been so focused on saving abused and neglected children, I haven't had time to immerse in international news. Why? What do you know?"

He gave a low whistle. "Holy hell. If the woman you helped find shelter is *El Chefe*'s woman, he won't give up until he takes her back to El Salvador or kills her. He won't hesitate to kill anyone who gets in his way."

"How do you know this?" Briana asked, rubbing her arms.

"I swear I read that once he sent a squad of men to his neighbor's house to shoot the neighbor, the children and the servants in that house because he got tired of listening to the dog bark, and the people never did anything to make it stop. He killed the family and had the dog brought to his place where he beat it until it didn't bark anymore."

Briana rubbed her hand across Lucy's shoulder, a frown pulling at her brow. "All because a dog barked?"

Rafe nodded. "I remembered the story because it seemed too bizarre to be true. I researched the issue and, sure enough, it was true. The guy's a sadistic bastard. He murdered an entire village because one man in that village skimmed a batch of the drugs they were producing and sold it to another cartel leader. Women, children…it didn't matter to him. He killed them all and burned the village to the ground."

Cold dread washed over Briana. "I'm glad we came to Montana. Surely, he won't have his men follow us here."

"If he does," Rafe said, "it'll be easier to see them coming than on a city street."

"What can I do to keep safe?" she asked, staring out the window at plains. "You can't always be around."

He frowned. "I plan on being around until the threat is neutralized."

"I know you will. But what if something happens to you? What if that bullet had hit you in front of the hotel? I had no way of defending myself."

Rafe glanced her way. "Do you know how to use a gun?"

She shook her head. "Dad took me to the gun range, once, before I went to college. He offered to buy me a gun, but I didn't feel comfortable enough to carry one."

"While we're out here, I'll teach you how to use one. You'll carry it and get to the point you feel better about having it near."

Her fists clenched. "I hate this. I hate that I've lost someone who meant so much to me. A senseless murder. They were after me. Now, I hate that I'm afraid. My daddy taught me to be cautious, not afraid. To be strong, not weak." She shook her head. "I hate this."

Rafe reached across the console and took one of

her fists in his large hand. "One good thing out of this, is that we're getting to know each other. We might have made new friends."

She unclenched her fist and wove her fingers into his. "There is that."

"We might never have met, otherwise," he said. "Not that I would've wished any of this to happen to you or your roommate."

She lifted his hand to her cheek, fighting back the ready tears. "Thank you for coming to my rescue. I don't know what I would've done if you hadn't."

"You probably would've kept driving." He chuckled. "You might have been in Texas by now, instead of Montana."

She smiled. "Probably. Not that I know anyone in Texas."

"Your brother is stationed there."

"Yeah. I guess I was headed that direction. But he wouldn't have been there."

"He cared enough to get you the help you needed." He brought her hand to his lips and brushed a kiss across her knuckles. "See the mountains ahead?"

She nodded, her gaze taking in the snow-covered peaks ahead.

"Those are the Crazy Mountains," Rafe said. "That's where we're headed."

"Why are they called the Crazy Mountains?" Briana asked.

"Legend has it that a family of settlers were

attacked by Blackfeet in the early eighteen hundreds. After her husband and children were killed, the mother went crazy and ran into the mountains. From that point on, the white settlers, and the Blackfeet, referred to the mountains as the Crazy Woman Mountains. The name has been shortened over time."

"That's sad," Briana murmured. Her heart hurt for the woman who'd witnessed the death of her husband and children. Two days ago, she might not have been able to relate with the woman's anguish. Having witnessed her roommate's death, she could understand.

"I think you have a friend in Lucy," Rafe said.

Briana glanced down at the dog, stirring at her feet. Lucy looked up at her with her big brown-black eyes. "She's beautiful."

"Did you have pets growing up?"

"We always had a couple of dogs in the house. They would alternate whose bed they would sleep in. On some nights, they'd sleep with Ryan, on others, with me. My parents were glad they didn't sleep with them."

"What kind of dogs were they?"

"We had a pair of miniature Shetland sheepdogs. Shelties." Briana smiled. "Sam and Trixie. They were with us for most of our young lives. They didn't pass until I left for college." She sighed. "I missed them terribly."

"College kept you busy?"

She nodded. "It was good to be running all the time. When I wasn't in class or studying, I worked at an ice cream shop part-time for extra spending money."

"What's your favorite ice cream?" he asked. "Or did you leave the ice cream business hating ice cream?"

She laughed. "I didn't eat ice cream for a solid year after I graduated. But I eventually came back to my favorite, Rocky Road. What's yours?"

"I'm boring. I love vanilla ice cream. But I like a thick hot fudge sauce poured over it."

"Mmm. You're making my mouth water." She looked out at the miles and miles of empty plains. "Do you know if Eagle Rock has an ice cream shop there?"

He shook his head. "I've never been to Eagle Rock. I just left the military and was on my way there when I got the call."

She gave him a grateful smile. "I'm lucky you were as close as you were. I doubt anyone would've gotten to me from Montana any sooner." She shivered. "What I don't understand is why they didn't attack me along the way? I was alone the entire trip from Joliet to Springfield. They had ample opportunity to run me off the road."

"I've been thinking about that," Rafe said. "Like we thought, it had to be your phone they followed. It might've taken them time to figure out where you were. They caught up while we were sleeping."

Briana trembled in the seat beside him. "I'm just glad the bullet missed."

"You and me both." Rafe smiled. "I have Lucy to thank for that. If I hadn't bent to pet her, I could've taken that bullet square in the chest."

"Do you think they'll hack into your phone's GPS now that they know I'm with you?" Briana asked.

"Hank sent me my cellphone before I left Texas. He said it has special security apps and encryption loaded into it to keep that from happening. We should be all right. And I haven't seen anyone following us since we ditched your phone in the back of that truck headed east from Springfield."

"I'll have to call the phone company and have my service cut off," Briana said.

"Another day. The less communication you have with your old life, the less of a chance *El Chefe* will have of finding you now."

Soon, they entered the foothills of the Crazy Mountains, zig-zagging along winding roads. They came to a town, the name posted on a quaint wooden sign, indicating they'd found Eagle Rock. Rafe didn't stop in the town.

"Shouldn't we stop for supplies?" Briana asked as they passed a small grocery store.

Rafe shook his head. "Hank said they had the cabin fully stocked and ready for us. Again, the less contact we have with others, the less chance of *El Chefe's* men finding us."

Briana nodded and brushed her hand over Lucy's smooth head. "I'm glad we stopped back in South Dakota for supplies for Lucy. I think we need to keep her on a lead until she gets used to us. If we let her run free, I'm afraid she'll try to find her way back to her owner's grave."

"Good idea. There have been dogs that have done that, finding their way across several states to get back to the home they were familiar with."

"Should we text Hank and let him know we're here?" Briana asked.

"He has access to my cellphone's location. He'll know. He said he'd head to the cabin when he saw we were near. Most likely, he'll be there before us."

Using the directions Hank had sent, they passed through town and out the other end, heading deeper into the mountains. Eventually, they turned off the paved road onto a gravel track, climbing up the side of a hill. The road wound through trees and around hills. When it forked south, Rafe turned north.

As they neared the top of a rise, the trees thinned. They emerged into a small clearing where a rustic log cabin perched in the middle. Beside it stood a shiny black pickup with a tall, dark-haired man and a petite, beautiful blond woman Briana found vaguely familiar. She carried a toddler on her hip, and her belly was swollen with a baby yet to come.

Rafe parked beside the pickup, climbed out and came around to help Briana and Lucy to the ground.

Lucy leaped out and ran to the end of her lead, eager to explore her new surroundings.

Briana was glad she'd snapped the leash onto her collar. She hated to think of the dog getting lost in the woods. She'd read about the bears that made their homes in the mountains and the wolves they'd reintroduced to the area. Lucy wouldn't stand a chance alone in the hills.

Rafe rested his hand at the small of her back as he led her over to where Hank stood with the woman and child.

Hank greeted Briana first. "You must be Briana Hayes. It's a pleasure to meet you. Your brother was very worried about your safety."

"Thank you for sending Rafe to help. I don't know what I would've done without him."

Hank shook Rafe's hand. "Welcome to the Brotherhood Protectors. Glad to have you aboard."

Rafe nodded. "I appreciate the opportunity."

Hank turned to the blonde. "This is my wife, Sadie."

Briana frowned. "Sadie...I feel like I should know you."

Hank chuckled. "You might know her for the all the movies she's made. Most people know her as Sadie McClain."

Briana blinked. "You're Sadie McClain, the movie star?"

She laughed. "I know. Out here, I don't look like I do on the big screen. I'm just Sadie, Hank's wife and Emma's mom." She looked down at the child in her arms. "This is Emma, our daughter."

Emma leaned toward Briana, her arms outstretched.

"Do you mind if I hold her?" Briana asked.

"Please," Sadie said. "She seems to want to go to you."

Briana handed the leash to Rafe and took Emma in her arms.

"You must have a way with children. She usually takes a minute or two to warm up to new people," Hank said.

"I'm good with the little ones," Briana said, smiling down at Emma in her arms. "It helps in my job. Doesn't it, Emma?"

"Your brother said you work with the Child Welfare Department in Chicago," Hank said.

Briana nodded.

"Is that how you got into trouble?" Hank asked.

"Not exactly," Briana said.

Sadie held out her arms. "Here, let me take Emma while you three talk."

Briana handed the child back to her famous mother, took a deep breath and launched into what had happened back in Chicago that had led her to her fleeing the city and traveling all the way out to Montana.

"Until he finds Alejandra, he won't leave Briana alone," Rafe concluded. "She's the key to where he can find his child."

"In the meantime, I'll fly some of my men to Illinois to bring Alejandra and her little girl here, where we can provide her the best of protection." Hank glanced at Sadie and Emma where they walked around the yard in front of the cabin. "I can imagine how terrified the woman is that she'll lose her child."

"There could be a problem with sending someone to Alejandra," Rafe said. "They know Briana's with me. They could link me to your company and follow anyone you send back to Illinois to Alejandra. They've already proven they can follow a cellphone." He frowned down at his. "Are you sure these phones are hack-proof?"

"Your phone isn't registered in your name. But it wouldn't hurt to ditch it now that you've come this far. I have a satellite phone in my truck. You can use it until we can get a burner phone for you to use. They're really hard to trace, and you can change out phones quickly and easily. For the time being, you can hole up in the cabin. We'll bring out anything you might need. If there are specific items of groceries you'd prefer, make a list and we'll get them for you, so you don't have to make the trip into town."

Briana gripped Hank's hand with both of hers.

"You don't know how much I appreciate all you've done for me."

"Are you going to go inside and see if there's anything you might need in the way of food or household goods? I shopped based on my tastes." Sadie smiled as she rejoined them. "You might not like what I like. I'm okay with that, but we'll need to get what you like on our next trip out."

"I'm sure it will all be fine," Briana smiled at the beautiful actress who looked as at home on the big screen as she did in the Crazy Mountains.

Sadie led the way into the cabin. "This is one of our hunting cabins. There's only one bed, but I had Hank bring a sofa in, in case you need another place to sleep."

She moved to the side with Emma and let Briana walk past her into the small space.

"I'm sorry, but it's rustic. And by rustic, I mean electricity. It has a generator to run the lights and the pump to get water. You'll be able to shower, but the stall is very small. Still, you won't have to use the old outhouse." Sadie grinned. "I don't mind roughing it, but I draw the line at outhouses."

Briana laughed. "It will be perfect."

"My computer guy, Swede, will dive into the dark web and see what he can find out about *El Chefe Diablo*'s activities," Hank said from behind her. "It might give us a heads-up on what he plans next."

Feeling a bit overwhelmed by all Hank and his

wife had done, Briana swallowed hard on the lump in her throat. "Thank you."

Sadie turned and hugged her. "I know how it feels to be scared. You don't know who to trust, where to turn and how to get out of a situation you didn't instigate. Hang in there. And if you need anyone to talk to, call me on the satellite phone."

"Speaking of which," Hank turned and left the cabin.

Rafe stepped across the threshold. "We should be safe here. It's far enough off the beaten path to discourage intruders from stumbling in."

Hank returned, holding a phone, which he handed to Rafe. "Based on what you told me about the weapons you own, I brought additional ammo and a small .40 caliber handgun for Briana."

Rafe smiled at Briana. "Good. We'll get right on those lessons."

Hank's jaw hardened. "Hopefully, she won't have to use it."

"Better to know how and not need it than need it and not know how to use it," Rafe said.

"Exactly." Sadie nodded. "I have my own little pistol. I take it out every week and shoot to keep up my skills."

Briana nodded. "That's what I'll have to do. First, I need to learn how to handle it."

"Look out, world." Rafe chuckled.

"Why are you laughing?" Briana demanded. "You're the one who'll be teaching me."

His face sobered so quickly, it was Briana's turn to laugh.

Her lips twisted. "See, it's not so funny when you're forced to teach the city girl how to shoot."

"That's not why I quit laughing. It is serious, and we need to start those lessons today."

"I'll get that gun and ammo," Hank said and ducked out of the cabin, again.

"I'd prefer to wait until Sadie and Emma are out of here," Briana said. "I don't want to scare them with my ineptitude."

"Oh, sweetie," Sadie grinned, "everyone has to start somewhere. But yes, the loud noises will scare Emma. We need to be going anyway. She'll be ready for a nap right after lunch. And I could use one, too." Sadie patted her perfectly rounded belly. "I find myself easily tired, these days."

A twinge of envy had Briana questioning her life choices. Soon, she'd be twenty-eight. She wasn't dating, didn't have a husband prospect, and she wasn't getting any younger.

Wasn't the big three-zero about the time her biological clock should start ticking? She'd known so many of her women friends who'd waited until they were in their thirties to have children, only to discover they'd waited too long. Some, even after long months of fertility treatments had yet to get pregnant. "When is your baby due?"

Sadie smiled. "Two months. But you'd think it was any day as big as I'm getting."

"You're all baby," Briana said.

Suddenly, Sadie's eyes widened. "Oh, well, there he goes, kicking me. I think he'll be a football player, as active as he is. Or maybe she'll go for hockey, as violently as she plays in my belly."

Hank stepped back through the door and handed a small case, and what appeared to be a shoulder holster, to Rafe. Then he dug in his front shirt pocket and his back jeans pockets for boxes of ammunition. "I'll bring more tomorrow. You'll burn through a lot, practicing. The good news is that there aren't any neighbors to disturb way out here."

"Sweetie, we need to get going," Sadie said, as Emma tugged on her hand. "Your daughter is restless."

Rafe set the gun, holster and bullets on the hand-hewn table and reached down to take Emma's hands. "Wanna come up with Uncle Rafe?"

Emma raised her arms without hesitation.

Rafe swung her up into the crook of his arm and walked with her out into the yard. "You need to come visit Uncle Rafe often."

"After the threat is past," Briana reminded him.

"After the mean ol' bad guys are gone," he said, blowing a raspberry on the toddler's belly.

Emma giggled and grabbed Rafe's ears.

"Hey, those are mine, and they don't come off easily." Rafe nuzzled the child's neck and blew a loud sound against her throat.

The toddler laughed and squirmed.

Briana watched, mesmerized by how easily the big Delta Force soldier interacted with the toddler.

"You're a natural, Rafe," Sadie said, echoing Briana's thoughts. "You don't have children, do you?"

"No. Never considered it. But I love playing with other people's kids. And they seem to like me." He grinned at the little girl in his arms. "You're a cutie," he said, "aren't you?"

"Come here, Emma." Hank reached for his daughter. "We need to get going before those giggles turn into angry squalling. She's a good baby, but she needs her recharge naps to keep those pretty lips smiling."

Hank settled Emma into the car seat in the middle of the back seat of his truck.

"If you come up with a list of items you'd like to have," Sadie said, "call us on the satellite phone. We'll pick them up in town and run them out to you."

"Thank you," Briana said. "I hate to ask for anything else. You've done so much already."

"Nonsense. We don't get that many visitors this far north. It's our pleasure to welcome the newcomers." Sadie gave Briana a hug. "I'm sorry about what happened to your friend. Just know, we're here if you need anything." Hank helped her up into the passenger seat and fastened her seatbelt around her, kissing her gently as he did.

Briana nodded, afraid to say anything lest it come out on a sob. The reminder of Sheila's death hit her, again.

Hank drove out of the yard and down the gravel path, leading away from the cabin, Rafe and Briana.

As the engine noise faded, silence wrapped around the little cabin in the mountains.

Lucy nudged Briana's hand, sliding under it. She leaned her fluffy black and white body against Briana's leg and whined softly.

"I know. It's really quiet out here."

Rafe snorted. "Wait until dark. Then every little sound will be like rockets going off. And you won't know what any of them are."

"You're not painting a calming picture for this city girl," Briana muttered.

He chuckled.

Briana wrapped the lead around her wrist and squared her shoulders. "Come on, Lucy. Let's explore our little patch of heaven."

Rafe joined her. "While we're at it, we can look for a place to set up our firing range."

"Good," she said. "The sooner I learn to fire a gun, the sooner I'll feel better about being out in the woods, far away from everything and everyone I ever knew."

Rafe slipped an arm around her waist and pulled

her close. "Not everyone you ever knew. You know me, now."

She leaned into his warmth and strength. "That's right. You're my friend." Her friend she was having more than friendly thoughts about. There could be a lot worse things than being alone on a mountain with a sexy former Delta Force soldier.

# CHAPTER 6

Rafe walked around the perimeter of the hilltop, checking out all the potential blind spots an enemy could leverage. While he explored, he found a sparsely treed hill not far from the cabin that would make a perfect backdrop for target practice.

He hurried back to the cabin, collected the weapons and left Lucy with bowls of water and dog food. With Briana, he returned to the hillside. They took advantage of the late afternoon sunshine to familiarize her with the .40 caliber HK pistol Hank had left for Briana.

Rafe set up several soft drink cans on a fallen log. Then he marched five long strides away from the target and motioned for Briana to join him. He handed her a pair of sponge ear plugs and showed her how to roll them between her thumb and fingers and stick them in her ears, where they expanded to fill the space.

She stood beside him, her hands clutched together in front of her. "I really don't know much of anything about shooting a gun," Briana said, staring at the .40 caliber pistol Rafe removed from the case.

"You'll learn," he said and went into describing each part of the weapon, how it worked and what could make it jam. He showed her how to hold it in her hands, balancing it on her opposite palm while it remained unloaded.

She listened carefully, asking questions and doing everything he said.

"You have to treat the weapon as if it were loaded at all times. Never point it at something, unless you intend to shoot it. If you're not shooting, point the barrel at the ground.

Then he had her face the cans and hold the gun out in front of her, her finger along the side of the trigger guard. "Now, switch the safety off, and place your finger on the trigger."

She thumbed the safety. "Like this?"

He nodded. "Yes. Finger on the trigger?"

"It is," she responded.

"Line up the sights like I showed you and pull the trigger by squeezing it gently until it clicks."

Her eyes narrowed as she looked down the top of the barrel and slowly squeezed the trigger. When it clicked, she flinched then relaxed.

Rafe grinned. "It's not so bad, is it? This weapon doesn't have much of a kick. You'll barely feel it jerk in your hand." He held out a full magazine. "Once we add the bullets, this weapon becomes lethal."

She nodded, drew in a deep breath and took the magazine from his hand.

"Slide it into the handle, while pointing the barrel at the ground. Not at your feet, but the ground in front of you. I don't know how many slap-happy recruits have blown off their toes because they weren't careful."

Her head shot up, her eyes rounding. "Really?"

He grinned. "No, but it pays to be super careful."

She nodded and slipped the magazine into the handle of the pistol.

Rafe stood at her left. "Now, do the same thing you just did with the empty gun. Aim down the sights at the target, and squeeze the trigger gently."

He stepped back and nodded. "You can do this."

Briana held the gun just as he'd shown her, switched off the safety and squeezed the trigger. The loud bang made her jump slightly.

The bullet hit the log below the can, sending splinters of rotted wood in all directions.

"That's good," he said.

"But I missed the can," she argued.

"You did, but only by hitting low. Aim a little high of the target this time."

She did and nicked the can, making it spin and

fall from the log. Briana laughed and glanced his way, her smile bright in the afternoon shadows.

They fired over a hundred rounds, adjusting her stance and the gun's sights, until Briana was comfortable with how the gun felt in her hands and she could consistently hit the target.

By the time they finished, the shadows had lengthened, and the sun had ducked behind the highest peak of the Crazy Mountains. Without the sun to warm the air, it got cold quickly.

Rafe helped Briana fit the shoulder holster over her arms and buckled it around her torso, his knuckles brushing against her breasts.

His groin tightened. "Sorry."

"Don't be," she said with a smile.

When she looked up at him, her gaze melted into his, making him even more aware of how close they were standing and how much he wanted to kiss her. But it was getting late.

"We need to get back to the cabin." Rafe took a step backward, shifting his gaze upward to the darkening sky.

Briana's chin dropped, and she fiddled with the straps around her arms before sliding the now empty pistol into the holster. "Lucy will be beside herself, thinking we left her."

"I was thinking more along the lines that this is bear country. Now that we're not shooting and making a lot of noise, they might come out of the woods to check things out."

"Bears?" Briana glanced around.

He nodded. "Let's get back so we can walk Lucy before it gets too dark to see."

Briana carried her gun case in her right hand.

Rafe carried his gun case in his left hand. He reached for her empty hand and curled his fingers around hers. "You did good today."

"I had the best instructor." She looked down at his hand holding hers. "Do you always hold hands with your students?"

He started to let go, but she tightened her grip. "No," he said. "But then I've never had as pretty a student as I did today."

She leaned against his arm. "Thank you for being patient with me. This is all new, but I'm sure I'll get the hang of it."

"You will. It just takes practice."

As they approached the cabin, Lucy started barking.

Rafe entered first, grabbing her by the collar and holding on long enough to snap the lead onto the metal loop. The border collie darted through the door and out into the yard, coming to an abrupt halt at the end of the long lead. Then she raced back to Briana and wagged her entire body at her feet.

Briana laughed and ruffled the collie's coat. "You have to wait for us, girl."

The three of them wandered around the perimeter of the yard until Lucy had done all of her business for the rest of the day.

When they returned to the cabin, Briana closed the door and let Lucy off her lead.

Rafe ducked back outside to start the generator and was back a couple minutes later.

Together, they went through the pantry staples Sadie had stocked the cabin with and settled on making chili.

"You can hit the shower while I cook." Rafe suggested.

"Are you sure?" she asked.

"Chili is about the only meal I can cook, besides steak on the grill. All the ingredients are here. I think I can handle the meal for tonight."

She smiled. "Deal. I'll come up with something for tomorrow night."

"Hopefully, we won't be here too many nights."

"I'm okay with it. I don't have any place else to go." Briana lifted her chin. "Besides, this is my chance to see some of Montana. Albeit a small corner of the Crazy Mountains. But what I've seen so far is stunningly beautiful."

Rafe nodded. "Agreed. One of these days, I want to try my hand at fly fishing in some of the mountain streams in the area."

"It could be one big vacation." Briana shook her

head. "If we didn't have a drug lord breathing down our necks."

"There is that little kink in our Montana getaway." He tipped his head toward the only other door besides the exit. "Go. The water should be hot by now."

He pulled cans from the shelves, plunked a pot on the gas stove and made chili, trying really hard not to think of Briana only a few feet away, naked in the shower. He could easily step into the bathroom and join her...if she wanted him to.

Rafe sighed. She was a client. They'd only known each other a little over twenty-four hours. He needed to keep his pants zipped and his hands to himself.

Protecting the beautiful Briana could be the toughest mission he'd ever been assigned.

BRIANA STRIPPED out of the clothes she'd worn for over forty-eight hours that now smelled like gunpowder and dog. The water pressure was questionable, but at least there was a shower in the cabin and she didn't have to find a creek in which to bathe. After shampooing her hair with the sweet-smelling shampoo Sadie had provided, she applied conditioner, and then scrubbed her body with the scented bodywash. Five minutes after entering the shower, she was clean, rinsed and feeling better than she had when she'd stepped in.

Several towels were folded neatly on a wooden shelf. Briana grabbed one and dried off. The chilly night air made her shiver in the small bathroom.

On another shelf, Briana was glad to find a stack of gently used clothes. They included a soft T-shirt and a pair of stretchy leggings she could wear the following day. She dug deeper, hoping to find a sexy nightgown. Had she really thought *sexy*? All she needed was a night gown or pajamas she could sleep in to save the clothes for the next day.

Sadly, there weren't any night clothes among the items, but there was a midnight-blue silk robe… She pulled on the robe that covered her down to the middle of her thighs. The silk was cool against her skin and made her shiver. Whether from cold or excitement, she didn't want to contemplate. After running a brush she found on the counter through her tangles, she left her hair hanging down around her shoulders to dry naturally. Other than the dark circles beneath her eyes, she didn't look too awful after having fled across the country. She looked at the stack of clothes and almost grabbed the T-shirt and leggings to cover her nakedness beneath the robe. Sadie had provided a brand-new package of sexy white lace panties, so at least Briana had those to wear beneath the robe. Firmly tying the sash around her waist, Briana left the bathroom and stood on the threshold, inhaling the rich, tantalizing scent of chili cooking on the stove.

Rafe sat on the couch, rubbing Lucy's neck. He looked up when Briana stepped through the door. He had opened his mouth to say something, but nothing came out.

Briana's cheeks heated at the hunger in Rafe's eyes. "Is dinner ready?" she asked, knowing the hunger had nothing to do with the fact they'd skipped several meals in their twenty-plus hours on the road from Illinois to Eagle Rock. Apparently, the robe was sexier than any leggings she could have worn.

Rafe nodded, cleared his throat and leaped to his feet. "Yes. Yes, it is. You can get started while I jump in the shower." He scooped chili into a bowl, added a spoon and set it on the table. "I'll only be a few minutes."

"That will give the chili time to cool a little. I'll wait for you," she said.

Rafe grabbed his duffle bag and ducked into the tiny bathroom.

Briana refilled Lucy's bowl of dog food and scratched her ears. "He's pretty cute, isn't he?"

Lucy looked up at her and whined softly.

"Yeah, he has that effect on me, too."

Briana spread out the blanket they'd purchased for Lucy across the wood floor.

Lucy circled several times, pawed at the fabric to arrange it just the way she liked it, and then dropped down and was asleep in seconds.

Less than five minutes later, Rafe stepped out of the bathroom, wearing jeans, a T-shirt draped around the back of his neck and nothing else.

Briana swallowed hard, her tongue suddenly dry. The man was built like a brick house. Muscles stretched across his broad chest then tapered down his torso to a narrow waist and hips. And then all that muscle flared out again over massive thighs. He padded barefooted across the floor to the pot on the stove and stirred it several times before he laid the spoon on the stove and shrugged into the T-shirt.

If she'd thought donning the shirt would make him any less sexy, she'd have been wrong.

The T-shirt stretched across his muscles, emphasizing rather than hiding them.

Swallowing hard again, Briana slipped onto the bench at the table and lifted her spoon, having a really hard time tearing her gaze away from Rafe.

"How's the chili?" Rafe asked, turning around with a bowl full for himself.

"What?" Briana glanced down at the bowl in front of her, heat rising up her neck to fill her cheeks. "Uh...I don't know. I was...waiting for you," she lied. She'd been admiring the way his shirt fit his shoulders and wishing she could lay her head on his chest and listen to the beat of his strong heart. Maybe then, she'd forget the reason why they were in Montana to begin with.

"Don't wait on me. Dig in." Rafe sat on the bench

across from her and dipped his spoon into the steaming chili.

Briana focused on the food in front of her, though her mind didn't lose sight of the man in her peripheral vision. She'd slept with him the night before, and he hadn't done anything more than hold her. What made her think he might want to do more than that?

Well, he had kissed her. Had it only been his way of comforting her?

Her gaze went to the only bed in the cabin and the couch. "I can sleep on the couch," she offered, taking a bite of the lukewarm chili.

His head came up. "That's not necessary. You can have the bed. I'll take the couch."

"It makes more sense for me to sleep on the couch. It's not long enough for you."

"I've slept in worse places," he said and scooped another spoonful of chili into his mouth.

"Or we could share the bed." Once again, her cheeks heated, and she looked down at the chili on her spoon. "I mean it's not like we haven't already slept together."

"True. But that was because you were scared and in shock."

"What if I'm the same tonight?" she asked. "But if it makes you uncomfortable…"

His lips twisted. "As a matter of fact, it did. After all, I'm a man. You're a beautiful woman."

"Never mind. I don't want you to do anything that

doesn't feel right to you." She ate another bite of chili though she had to swallow hard to make it go down.

He lowered his spoon and captured her gaze with his. "Sweetheart, it felt too right to me. I'm just not sure it's the right thing for you."

She tilted her head. "Why?"

"I wanted a whole lot more than to simply hold you all night. Not that I didn't enjoy that."

"Oh," she said.

"Wait until we call it a night. You can make the decision then. I don't mind the thought of sleeping in a real bed versus a lumpy couch."

Briana finished the food in her bowl and helped clean the small kitchenette, standing beside Rafe as he dipped dishes into soapy water then rinsed them thoroughly, before handing them to her to dry.

They bumped into each other several times, sending shocks of electricity throughout Briana's body. The longer they worked side by side, the more aware Briana became of the soldier.

Still distracted, she turned to hang the dishtowel on a hook on the wall and spun, running into the solid wall of Rafe's chest.

His hands came up to rest on the swell of her hips, long enough to steady her.

"Sorry."

"I'm not," he whispered, his tone even, deep and sexy as hell. He cupped her face in his palm and bent, lowering his head and face to within a fraction of an inch from hers. "I don't know what it is about you that makes me want to kiss you."

"Is that a bad thing?" she asked.

"Yes. It makes me vulnerable."

Her brow furrowed. "But you're so strong and courageous."

"Strength isn't just about the muscles. Find a man's Achilles heel, and you can take him down with a pinch." His lips hovered over her mouth, his warm breath tempting her. "Tell me no, and I'll back off."

"I can't," she whispered, her body burning in anticipation. "I want you to kiss me, too."

"It could lead to so much more. I'm not sure I can stop once I start down that path."

"Do you need me to lead the way?" Her gaze shifted from his mouth to his eyes. His dark brown irises smoldered to black.

"I'm willing to follow," he breathed against her lips.

The first night they were together, all he'd done was hold her as they'd rested in the same bed. Yes, Briana wanted him to hold her. And she wanted so much more. Sliding her hands up his chest, she laced them behind his neck and raised up on her toes, closing the distance between them.

When her lips touched his, his arms slipped around her back and crushed her to him, his mouth claiming hers in a kiss that shook her to her very core.

Briana opened to him, meeting his tongue with hers in a sensuous caress that started a fire low in her belly and burned outward. She pressed her body to his, the silk of her robe sliding across her skin, reminding her that she was almost naked beneath. All she had to do was release the belt and let it fall to the floor.

Rafe lifted his head and stared down into her eyes. "I didn't take this job to seduce my client."

"Would it make you feel better if I seduce you?" she asked, a smile pulling at the corners of her lips. She stepped back, released the belt on the robe and let it slide off her shoulders. The silk floated down her body to pool at her ankles. All she had on were the lacy panties and a tentative smile.

*Please, like what you see.*

For a long moment, he stared into her eyes. Then his gaze swept down her body. Rafe drew in a deep breath, bent, scooped her up into his arms and carried her to the only bed in the one-room cabin.

When he reached it, he set her on her feet, cupped the back of her neck with one hand, and kissed her slowly, as if savoring the taste of her.

Briana slipped her hands between them, bunched her fingers into his shirt and tugged it from the waistband of his jeans.

Rafe stepped back, yanked his T-shirt from around his neck and tossed it over the end of the bed.

Meanwhile, Briana loosened the buckle on his

belt and pulled it free of the loops on his jeans. She pushed the button loose and slid his zipper down. Then she reached inside and cupped him over his boxer briefs, feeling the swell of his cock, hard and thick against her fingers, nothing but the cotton of his briefs between them.

Blood rushed through her body, her pulse pounding through her veins.

Rafe shoved his jeans down his legs, kicking free of the denim.

Finally naked, he stood before her in all his masculine glory. "Are you sure about this?"

She nodded, her breath too tight in her lungs to push air past her vocal cords.

Rafe bent to retrieve his wallet from his jeans and plucked a condom from inside.

Briana took the packet from him, tore it open and rolled the rubber down his engorged shaft, pausing to palm his balls before withdrawing her hand.

With a sexy growl, Rafe hooked his thumbs into the elastic band of the lace panties and dragged them down over her legs. He dropped to one knee and followed the path of the panties, pressing his lips to the inside of her thighs, licking the curve of her knee and tugging the lace free of her ankles.

Completely deficient of air, her breath hitched in her lungs. Briana couldn't move, couldn't resist.

As he rose, he dragged his fingers up her legs to cup her sex, a finger stroking her damp entrance.

Briana sucked in a breath and released it on a moan.

Rafe slipped his hands over the swells of her ass and lifted; she wrapped her legs around his waist.

With her hands resting on his broad shoulders, Briana lowered herself onto his thick shaft, her slick channel accepting him.

He filled her, sliding deep inside until he was fully sheathed.

For a long moment, he didn't move, giving her body time to adjust to his girth before he gripped her hips and lifted her, sliding out of her to the very tip of his cock.

Sensations rushed over her like fireworks bursting throughout her body.

When he pulled free of her, she cried out.

"Shhh," he murmured as he laid her on the bed and crawled up between her legs, leaning on his arms, a hand positioned on either side of her head. "I want to explore all of you."

And he proceeded to do just that, starting with her mouth. He kissed her, summoning her tongue to dance with his. When they needed to breathe again, he swept his lips across her chin and down the length of her neck to tongue the pulse beating rapidly at the base. From there, he trailed kisses and nips across her collarbone, over the swell of her breast to the hardened nipples puckered and ready for whatever he had in mind.

He took one between his lips and scraped his teeth across it.

Briana arched her back against the mattress, pressing her breast deeper.

He sucked inward, taking as much as he could inside his warm, moist mouth, flicking the tip with his tongue until Briana moaned and writhed beneath him.

Moving to the other breast, he massaged it with his fingers, then sucked at the nipple pulling hard, igniting Briana's insides with a desire so strong she couldn't wait for him to go lower.

And he did.

Abandoning her breasts, he tongued and nibbled his way across her ribs, dipping briefly into her belly-button and, finally, arriving at the puff of hair covering her sex.

Parting her legs wider, Briana raised her hips, wanting him inside her, the sooner the better. "Please," she moaned.

"Please, what?" he said, his breath stirring her curls, making her ache with longing.

"I want more. I want you inside me," she said, her fingers curling into the comforter.

Rafe chuckled, parted her folds and dipped a finger into her wet channel, swirling around, making her crazy.

He slid the damp finger up between her folds and stroked the tender nubbin of flesh.

Briana gasped, her body tensing; her breath lodged in her throat.

He flicked that flesh and rubbed it again.

"Oh, sweet Jesus," she called out.

"Like that?" he asked, blowing a warm stream of air over her damp clit.

"Oh, yes!" She lay back against the pillow, her head rocking side to side. "Don't stop."

"I won't. Not until you're completely satisfied."

"*Yesss.*"

He slipped his finger back inside her and lowered his head to take that nub of flesh between his lips and suck gently. When he released her, he flicked her there, tonguing and tapping, swirling and sucking, until she exploded into a thousand sparkling lights. Her body shook with the force of her release, pulsing and thrumming as she rode the wave to the very end.

Still, it wasn't enough. She wouldn't be completely satisfied until she had him buried deeply inside her.

Lacing her fingers in his hair, she tugged gently, urging him upward.

He licked her one last time then climbed up her body and settled between her legs, the tip of his cock nudging her entrance.

Briana reached low, captured the swells of his taut ass and brought him home. He filled her, sliding deep inside, his cock pressing against the walls of her channel, fitting her so perfectly, she felt as if the two of them made one.

When he moved, he set off an entirely different charge of electricity zipping through her body.

He pumped in and out of her. She dug her feet into the mattress and met him thrust for thrust. The bedsprings squeaked and the headboard banged against the wall with the force of their efforts.

On the way up to her second orgasm for the night, Briana felt Rafe tense, his body grow tight and his breath catch. He thrust one last time, sending her catapulting over the edge.

He held steady, his cock buried so deep inside her, she couldn't tell where he ended, and she began. His shaft pulsed within her as he came. For a long moment he leaned over her, his head thrown back, his jaw tight. Then he dropped down on her, stealing the breath from her lungs with the weight of his body.

Briana didn't care if she ever breathed again. She loved how he felt, crushing her beneath him.

Then he gathered her in his arms and rolled the two of them onto their sides, retaining their intimate connection. He pulled one of her legs up over his thigh and rested his hand on her naked hip.

Briana rested her head on Rafe's arm and circled one of his hard brown nipples with the tip of her finger, loving that they were still together in the most intimate of ways.

It felt so natural and right, she didn't feel at all embarrassed. "I know I'm just a client to you, so I don't expect anything from tonight." She glanced up at him. "No strings."

His arms tightened around her, and a frown settled between his eyebrows. "Damn, woman. How can you talk like that when we're lying here like this?" He pulled her closer. "And you're not just a client. You think I would do this with every client?"

She shrugged. "I don't want you to think I'll be needy. You have your life here in Montana. I have a life back in Chicago." She sighed. "I had a life back in Chicago. I like to think I was making a difference."

"Sweetheart, you're making a difference in my life, right now."

She looked up into his eyes. "How so?"

He brushed a strand of her hair back behind her ear. "I left the army because I felt like something was missing in my life. I didn't know what it was…until I met a woman over the phone, and we talked for hours getting to know each other."

"We did talk for a long time," she said, her fingers sliding over his shoulder, loving how smooth his skin was and how hard the muscles were beneath it.

His gaze narrowed, capturing hers. "The point is, you showed me what I was missing."

"And what was that?" she asked, her breath catching and holding in her chest.

"Connection. And it's more than having a date, it's

more than sex. All we did was talk. And I felt more connected to life, and what I want out of it, than I'd felt in a very long time… Hell, ever."

She laughed softly and stared at his chest. "I'd say we're even more connected, now. But I don't want you to think I'm a clingy woman. Being confined together can make people think there's more to their relationship than really exists."

He tipped her chin up, forcing her to look him square in the eyes. "Is that how you feel?"

She lifted a shoulder. "I don't know how I feel," she said, though she really did. However, she wasn't prepared to admit it.

"Tell you what. Let's leave tomorrow to tomorrow and concentrate on today," he said. "Do you want to be with me today?"

She nodded. "Yes. Do you want to be with me?"

He smiled down at her, and his cock hardened inside her. "Yes. And I think you know it."

Her heart fluttered at the sexy way his lips curled. She slid her leg down his thigh and then back up to curl around his hip. "Are you tired?"

He shook his head. "Not in the least. Are you?"

She shook her head and pushed him onto his back, rolling with him so that she was straddling his hips. She bent to claim his lips with a soul-searing kiss. When she came up, she gave him what she hoped was a sexy smile and practically purred, "My turn to drive."

# CHAPTER 7

RAFE WOKE to the sound of Lucy whining. When he sat up, the room was so dark, he couldn't see the dog much less the hand in front of his face. Before they'd gone to sleep, he'd turned off the battery-powered lantern, plunging them into the inky blackness of a night in the deep woods, far away from nightlights plugged into electrical sockets or streetlights shining through windows.

In the Crazy Mountains of Montana, they had neither streetlights nor electricity, unless he fired up the generator again.

"Why's Lucy whining?" Briana rolled over and pressed her warm breasts against his back.

He wanted nothing more than to pull her naked body into his arms and make love to her again.

Lucy barked, cutting that fantasy short.

"I'll take her out for a walk," he said.

"You can turn on the lantern. It won't bother me," she said and yawned. "Want me to go with you?"

"No. I'll be right back. I'm sure she just wants to relieve herself. I shouldn't be long. You can stay here and keep the bed warm."

He turned on the lantern, pulled on his jeans, boots and a jacket and snapped the lead on Lucy's collar.

By then, Lucy was pacing in front of the door, whining and sniffing.

"She must need to go really badly." Briana sat up in the bed, pulling the sheet over her naked breasts.

His cock twitched and grew hard in an instant. "I'll be right back," he said, opened the door and stepped out into the night.

The moon and starlight provided enough light he didn't need the lantern; he could see almost as well as he could during the day.

Lucy took off, straining at the leash, growling low in her chest.

"What's wrong, girl?" Rafe asked. He hadn't taken three steps from the cabin when he remembered this was bear and wolf country. About the time he decided to turn around and get his gun, Lucy went berserk, barking like a mad dog. It was all Rafe could do to hold her back. He tried dragging her in, but she twisted and jerked at the leash, making it impossible for Rafe to pick her up and carry her back inside.

Rafe had just grabbed Lucy by the scruff of her

neck when a bear burst out of the shadowy tree line, rose up on his hind legs and lumbered toward them, roaring. Moonlight glittered off his long, wickedly sharp teeth.

Barking fiercely, Lucy broke free of Rafe's hold and lunged toward bear.

The lead pulled tight, catching her up short. She flipped over, turned, and then tried again to get to the bear.

Without a gun in his hand, Rafe couldn't help her. And he couldn't drop the lead and run back into the cabin. He reeled the dog in, pulling on the long lead, one foot at a time, the dog's lunging motions making it almost impossible.

The bear followed as if being lured by the promise of a snack, roaring and swiping at the air with its massive paw.

The bear was almost on Lucy. Rafe could smell the animal and feel the heat of his massive body. He didn't fear for himself, but he worried that he wouldn't get Lucy away from the beast before he swiped her with his heavy paws and razor-sharp claws.

Just when the bear pulled his paw back to deliver a killing blow, a low bang sounded behind Rafe.

He ducked and spun toward the cabin.

Briana stood in the doorway, her silk robe hanging open over her naked body, holding the pistol she'd practiced shooting the day before.

"Get out of here," she yelled.

The bear roared, the sound ripping through the night air.

Lucy strained at the leash, barking so much her voice went hoarse.

Briana fired again, aiming over all of their heads.

Rafe ducked low, dragging Lucy toward him.

The bear dropped to all four feet, turned and ran into the woods, grumbling as he went.

Lucy tried to follow, but now she was close enough, Rafe grabbed her around her middle and carried to the cabin.

Briana backed into the cabin, pointing the gun at the ground. "Holy shit, Rafe. Holy shit."

Rafe carried Lucy through the door and kicked it shut behind him before he dropped her on her feet.

Briana's face was chalk white, and her eyes rounded. She trembled from head to toe. "Did you see that bear?"

He chuckled, took the gun from her shaking hands, dropped the magazine out of the handle, cleared the chamber and laid it on the table. Then he pulled her into his arms and held her tight. "Thank you for having the foresight to bring a gun with you."

"He was so close."

"Yes, he was." So close, Rafe had felt his breath when he'd roared. "That was some quick thinking on your part."

"I got up as soon as you left, thinking you might

need a gun. Everyone says this is bear country." She looked up into his eyes. "Holy hell. It is."

"He's gone. I think he was more scared of you than you were of him." He smoothed the hair back from her forehead. "You were amazing. Fierce."

"Terrified," she whispered. "It almost got you and Lucy."

"But it didn't." He tipped her chin up. "Because of you."

"I almost forgot to flip the safety off."

"But you did." He kissed the tip of her nose.

"I did it," her lips curved into a tremulous smile, "didn't I?"

"Yes, you did." He pulled her close, slipping his hands inside the silk of her robe and rubbed his hands over her smooth skin. "Thank you for saving Lucy and me." He held her close, his cock hardening as her naked breasts pressed against his chest. He shrugged out of his jacket and draped it over the bedpost. Then he scooped her up into his arms, carried her to the bed and made sweet love to her.

They slept until the sun shone through the only window and Lucy insisted on going outside to relieve herself.

Rafe was more prepared this time, taking his gun in the shoulder holster. He was still kicking himself for being so clueless the night before. Making love to Briana seemed to have sucked his brain free of all braincells. He'd have to be more aware and stay on his toes. The bear could have been *El Chefe*'s hired thugs, and he'd have had less of a chance of surviving them. They'd have shot him on sight. From now on, he'd have to take all the precautions. For that matter, he might want to set out some kind of early warning system to alert them to incoming intruders.

With nothing but time on their hands, they could come up with something.

He left Briana in bed while he walked Lucy around the cabin looking for places he could rig a trip line of something like cans filled with rocks that would rattle when someone ran over the line. Hell, he could ask Hank if he had some kind of early warning or security system that ran on batteries. He could use it for people as well as for angry grizzly bears. Then he wouldn't be surprised in the middle of the night when he'd rather be in bed making love to Briana.

When he came back into the cabin, Briana had omelets made of fresh farm eggs, canned ham and minced onion. As they ate, they talked about the bear, Lucy and what they might do for the rest of the day. They settled on clearing away brush from the nearby tree line to allow them to see more clearly into the shadows and to disallow the enemy, or bears, to move in so closely, undetected.

Rafe contacted Hank via the satellite phone, requesting something in the way of a surveillance system that ran on batteries and would provide some kind of warning should man or beast approach the cabin

At the end of the day, Hank arrived with a tall, broad-shouldered man with a shock of light blond hair.

"Donovan, this is Axel Swenson, Navy SEAL, and the brains behind the Brotherhood Protectors," Hank said.

"Hank's the brain. I just work the electronics and computers." The blond-haired man held out his hand. "Call me Swede."

Rafe shook the man's hand. "Nice to meet you, Swede."

Rafe turned to Briana. "This is Briana Hayes. My...client." He got stuck on the word. Already, Briana was so much more than a client. He was afraid he was falling for her. Never in all his thirty-four years had he felt the way he did about another woman. Hell, he didn't trust most women. His mother had barely given a damn about him. None of the women he'd gone out with had held his attention for more than a night in bed, and he doubted they would've shot at a bear to save his life. Yeah, Briana was different. Still, he wasn't sure how things would play out between them when the threat went away. He had a job in Montana. She would move back to Chicago and do good things for the children there.

"We brought you the surveillance equipment you requested. The cameras run on batteries and will also work on infrared at night. We can set up a way to check them using a battery-powered unit you can recharge when you have the generator running."

Rafe helped unload the boxes from the truck and laid them out on the tailgate. Soon, they had cameras positioned all around the perimeter of the cabin, and the base unit installed with a monitor on the table inside.

When they were all done setting up, they tested with Hank and Swede walking out by the units. Each time, a signal sounded, alerting Briana and Rafe to intruders.

Hank and Swede returned to the cabin and dug out another device for them to use to monitor their location—a drone they could operate to give them a birds-eye view of the road and land leading up to the cabin. Swede showed Rafe and Briana how to operate it and had them practice a couple of times before he was satisfied they could handle it.

Before Hank climbed into his truck to leave, he fished in his pocket and pulled out a silver necklace with a gemstone pendent. "Briana, I'd like you to wear this necklace at all times, even when you're in the shower or swimming. It's got a GPS tracking device embedded beneath the gemstone. If you're kidnapped, or even just lost in the woods, we'll be able to locate you by computer or one of the hand-held tracking devices we have back at the ranch. Also, I wanted you to know my guys made it to Illinois. They'll move Alejandra from the shelter to a safe house here in Montana sometime in the next forty-eight hours."

Briana frowned. "The more people who know where she is, the greater chance someone will slip up and reveal her whereabouts."

Hank shook his head. "My guys are all special forces. They know how to keep their mouths shut and how to slip in and out of places without being detected. You can trust them completely."

Briana chewed on her bottom lip. "I promised Alejandra she'd be safe."

"And she will be," Hank said. "And we'll keep you safe, as well."

"I'm not as worried about me as much as I am about Alejandra and her baby," Briana said. "Will you let me know when you get her moved into the safe house?"

"I will," Hank said. "One last thing." He reached into the back seat of the truck and removed a cooler, handing it to Rafe. "Sadie sent out some ranch-raised beef steaks for you two to enjoy, plus a bottle of her favorite wine. She cooked the potatoes, and the steaks are medium rare. All you need to do is warm them up. She included a green salad, dressing and two pieces of apple pie. I told her she'd better have some left for me when I get home, or I'll stay and eat with the two of you." He winked. "Enjoy and try not to get eaten by the bear."

Hank and Swede left, driving away as the sun slipped below the mountaintops, casting them into shadow.

Rafe carried the cooler to the cabin and waited while Briana and Lucy entered before he followed. "I don't know about you, but roughing it in the Crazy Mountains ain't all that bad."

Briana grinned. "It could be a heck of a lot worse. We have running water, great food and good company. What more could we ask for?"

Rafe's grin faded. "For *El Chefe* to back off and leave you alone. I'd feel better if we had an end in sight. We don't know if he'll give up trying to find you, or by some miracle, locate you here in the Crazy Mountains. I'd almost rather confront him than be forever in limbo."

She shrugged. "I look at this as time I get to spend with you. And now that we have the surveillance system, we can relax a little."

Rafe nodded. He'd let her think they'd be just fine with an early warning system. Truth was, until *El Chefe* backed off, they had to be hyper-aware at all times. Surveillance system or not, if the drug lord sent enough men in to extract Briana, they could be overrun before Hank and his team had time to provide backup.

Rafe hoped it didn't come to that. In the meantime, they had a wonderful meal and another night together. Life could be a whole lot worse. He could be stuck with a client he couldn't stand instead of Briana, a woman he was quickly learning to like a little too much.

But then, what was too much? She was an amazing woman. The kind of woman he could see himself staying with for a very long time.

# CHAPTER 8

AFTER THE MEAL Hank and Sadie had provided, Rafe and Briana walked Lucy outside once more before calling it a night.

They made love until midnight and fell asleep in each other's arms. The bear didn't return that night, and nothing set off the alarms, allowing them a full night's sleep.

Briana woke the next day fully refreshed and ready to do something with the day. She suggested they take the drone higher up the mountain and get a feel for the terrain around the cabin. Rafe agreed, and they packed a picnic lunch and the drone, snapped a leash on Lucy and spent the day tromping through the hills, getting to know each other better and laughing a lot.

She learned she was pretty good at operating the drone. Her hands were more adept at subtle changes in direction than his, and she maneuvered the drone all around the hilltop where the cabin perched.

Lucy chased rabbits and drank from mountain streams full of clear, cold water from snow melt.

The day was idyllic, the sun shone down on them, and they didn't see a single bear or bad guy. Just her, Rafe and Lucy in the beautiful Montana mountains. She could almost believe it was a vacation. And she loved everything about Rafe. He was smart, understood how to get around in rough terrain and took good care to make sure she didn't walk off a cliff or fall into a ravine.

By the end of the day, she was gloriously tired and happy. Which felt strange, considering she was on the run from a drug lord, the head of a cartel in El Salvador, who had contacts and thugs he could tap into in the States. Who knew how far his reach extended? She should be more afraid, but it was hard to be when she had Rafe with her and she was surrounded by the beauty of the Montana mountains.

They spent another night in each other's arms, making love until after midnight. Early the next morning, they were awakened by the buzzing of the satellite phone.

Rafe rolled out of the bed and padded barefooted across to the table to answer. "Donovan here."

He listened for a few minutes, and then nodded.

"I'll tell her... We will. Let us know if you have any trouble. Yes, sir. Out here."

"Did they get Alejandra moved?" Briana leaned up on an elbow, letting the sheet slide down to expose her breasts. She hoped it would be enough to make Rafe come back to bed and make love to her again. They'd have to add condoms to the list of supplies they needed Hank and Sadie to pick up in town.

That would be awkward.

"Hank said they have Alejandra in a safe house here in Montana with a couple of his guys providing round-the-clock protection. They flew her out on a private plane in the middle of the night and landed in the dark. She and the baby are safe. He wants us to be extra vigilant."

A knot formed in Briana's gut. "Why do we need to be *extra* vigilant? The way I see it, you don't need to protect me now. I don't know where Alejandra is hiding. I couldn't tell *El Chefe* even if I wanted."

Rafe laid down in the bed beside her and gathered her in his arms. "You know that, and I know that, but *El Chefe Diablo* doesn't. As far as he knows, you're the only one who knows where Alejandra is hiding."

"Then we can just tell him I don't know anymore. That she's gone from the location where I left her."

"He may or may not believe you. And if he does believe you, he might want revenge against you for interfering in the first place. And if we contact him, he might figure out where you are. We can't risk that."

Briana sighed. "How long can I hide from this man? It doesn't make any sense. Maybe we need to come out in the open and flush out his minions."

Rafe pressed his lips to hers. "No."

"I can't live like this forever. I have a job. A life."

"And he could snuff it out in a heartbeat."

She captured his face between her palms. "Seriously, as much as I love being with you, I can't live like this forever. You can't protect me forever."

"Are you tired of me already?" Rafe leaned over her and kissed her forehead, her cheeks and her nose.

Her pulse quickened, and an ache built deep down in her core. "Far from it. But we have to be real."

Rafe kissed a path down her neck, across her collarbone and lower to claim one tightly budded nipple.

"Are you listening to me?" she asked, her voice more of a moan.

"I'm listening," he said and sucked the nipple into his mouth.

God, the things he was doing to her made her come apart at the seams. She tried to focus. "Life has to go on."

"Can it wait until after we make love?" he asked, as he switched to the other breast.

"Rafe," she started to argue, but the air left her

lungs as his hand slipped over her belly to cup her sex.

"Yes, Briana?" he said and blew a warm stream of air over her damp nipple. "I'm here." Rafe kissed her nipple and moved lower to her rib. "And here." He kissed another rib. "And here."

"Oh, who am I kidding?" She gave up and made love to him in broad daylight with Lucy lying on the floor in front of the door. If *El Chefe Diablo* was coming for her, she'd at least have enjoyed the time she spent with Rafe. When it was all over, she'd go back to Chicago, and he'd go on to his next assignment with the Brotherhood Protectors.

After they made love, they lay for a long time in each other's arms, while birds sang outside, and sunshine streamed through the single window.

"I'll miss this, when it's all over," she whispered.

"Why should you miss this?" he asked.

Before she could answer, an alarm went off on the surveillance system.

Rafe sprang from the bed, grabbed his handgun and ran to the video monitor. He studied the six display windows on the screen. One had a red outline. In the display image stood a four-legged animal.

Lucy paced at the door but didn't whine or bark.

After several minutes staring at the monitor, Rafe was joined by Briana, pulling her robe around her. "Anything?"

"An elk and her baby." He pointed to the red-rimmed image.

Briana laughed. "Better them than the bear." She handed him his jeans. "Come on, let's go for a walk. Lucy needs some exercise."

They spent the day wandering over the hills, returning to the cabin before the sun sank below the ridgeline. They fed Lucy, ate dinner and settled in to read books Sadie and Hank had left on a shelf beside the canned goods.

When it was time for bed, they made love until late in the night. Sometime later, Lucy whined at the door to be let out. Rafe dressed in jeans, boots and his jacket, tucked his handgun into his pocket and checked the monitor for any blinking lights. The infrared display showed nothing amiss. He snapped the lead on Lucy's collar and let himself out through the door. "Lock it behind me," he said.

Briana locked the door behind him and shivered in the cool mountain air. She pulled on a pair of leggings and a T-shirt, and then slipped her feet into her shoes and wandered over to the surveillance monitor. An alert went off, and one of the screens blinked red.

Her pulse leaped as she studied the monitor. In the blinking square, she could see the infrared image of Rafe and Lucy walking near the edge of the clearing. She smiled as they stopped to let the dog sniff at every little thing on the ground.

Lucy had seemed to settle in with them, glad for the attention and love she'd missed with the passing of her previous owner.

As Briana watched, Lucy braced herself, lowered her head and bared her teeth.

At the same time, another alarm went off on the surveillance system. Briana expected it to be from the camera closest to the one near Rafe and Lucy as they crossed into its sector.

However, the screen that lit up wasn't from the cameras closest to Rafe and Lucy. It was from a camera on the back side of the cabin.

Briana leaned closer to the monitor, studying the image. At first, she didn't see anything, but then a white silhouette pushed up from the ground and moved toward the cabin. Another white silhouette rose up and followed the first. They were hunkered over, and when they straightened, Briana could tell they were people, and they were carrying guns. A third alarm went off and another screen blinked with a red outline. More men emerged from the trees, running toward the cabin.

Her heart leaped into her throat. She had to warn Rafe before they reached him and Lucy.

Briana reached for her pistol, slammed the magazine into the handle and ran for the door.

# CHAPTER 9

As soon as Lucy took up a defensive stance and growled, Rafe stiffened, yanked his gun out of his jacket and started back toward the cabin.

Before he reached it, headlights blinked on, and vehicles raced up the drive and through the trees, heading directly for him and Lucy.

He ran, but he wasn't going to make it to the cabin. Not before the vehicles reached him first. He prayed Briana would stay in the cabin with the door locked and call Hank on the satellite phone. Hank wouldn't get there in time to help, but he might catch up to them before they disappeared with Briana.

When he realized he wouldn't reach the cabin in time, he released Lucy's lead and told the dog, "Go, Lucy!"

The dog ran into the woods.

Rafe turned, braced his handgun in his palms and

fired at the headlights and the tires, hoping to slow the lead vehicle.

A dark Jeep with its top off barreled toward him.

Rafe fired in the direction of the driver, but the vehicle didn't slow. At the last minute, Rafe threw himself to the side, hit the ground, rolled and came up on his feet. Another Jeep raced up to him. A man leaned out the side of the vehicle and hit Rafe in the side of the head with a baseball bat.

Pain knifed through his head, and Rafe fell to his knees, the gun slipping from his hand. Another man leaped out of the vehicle and ran toward him with a club like what the policemen carry. When he cocked his arm to hit Rafe with it, a flash of black and white leaped out of the tree line.

Lucy grabbed the man's arm before he could swing it at Rafe and bit down hard.

The man screamed and flung his arm backward, knocking Lucy away.

Rafe felt the ground, searching desperately for the pistol. When his fingers curled around it, he staggered to his feet and aimed at the man trying to hit the dog with the club.

As Rafe leveled his weapon and took aim, the man swung hard and hit Lucy in the head.

The border collie yelped and crumpled to the ground, lying still.

Rafe pulled the trigger too late to save the dog.

The man with the club tipped sideways and collapsed, unmoving in the dust.

His head spinning and a gray cloud closing in on all sides, Rafe turned back to the cabin. The lead Jeep had come to a halt in front of the door, and four men jumped to the ground.

"Briana, don't come out!" he yelled.

Two men raced up beside Rafe and grabbed his arms. Through the gray cloud, he fought them, swinging and missing. When one of them coldcocked him in the jaw, he hit the ground, his vision blacking out for a moment. Long enough for the men to grab his gun, yank his arms behind his back and slap a zip-tie around his wrists.

They jerked Rafe to his feet, dragged him to the lead Jeep, and stood him in front of the headlights.

"Briana Hayes, if you want this man to live, come with us," a man in a black leather jacket and a ski mask called out.

"Don't," Rafe shouted.

The man beside him slammed a meaty fist into his gut.

Rafe doubled over, fighting back the black abyss threatening to consume him.

The man in the black leather jacket waved a pistol toward Rafe. "Bring him closer."

The two men on either side of him dragged him forward.

The man in the leather pointed his gun at Rafe's

head. "You have until the count of three to come out or the man dies."

The door remained closed.

*Briana, don't.* Too dizzy to form words, Rafe hung between the two men, praying Briana didn't cave in to their demand.

"One... You really want to watch his head splattered all over the ground? Two...I ain't shittin' you. It's your decision. You want him to die?"

"Wait!" Briana's voice called out through the wood-paneled door. "How do I know you'll let him live?"

"You don't. We'll get you one way or another. But you have my word we won't kill him if you come with us without a fight."

Briana snorted. "The word of a thug?"

"It's the best you'll get. You don't have much choice either way."

"Let him go, and I'll come out," Briana said.

"No," Rafe said.

Again, he was punched in the gut, knocking the wind out of him.

"Don't hurt him. I'm coming out," Briana cried.

Rafe tried to tell her no, but he couldn't get air past his vocal cords.

The men holding his arms were the only reason he hadn't fallen on his face. He hated that he couldn't fight back, that they were outnumbered, and that Briana was giving up her freedom to save his sorry ass. He should have been more prepared. He should have been ready.

But they'd never expected *El Chefe* would send an army of men to secure one woman when he'd only sent one before.

The cabin door opened, and Briana stepped out, her hands raised in the air. "Don't shoot him. I'll go with you. Just let him live."

The man in the black leather jacket tilted his head toward the Jeep. "Get in the back."

Briana walked toward the Jeep, her brow furrowed, her gaze on Rafe. "Don't hurt him," she said as she climbed into the backseat.

Two men got in with her, one on either side.

The man in the leather jacket slid into the passenger seat, and his driver got behind the steering wheel.

"What do you want us to do with him?" one of the men holding him up asked.

"Leave him," their leader said. "Maybe the bears will eat him and put him out of his misery."

The men on either side of him shoved him to the ground and left him lying there as they grabbed their guy on the ground, leaped into their Jeep and followed the lead vehicle out of the yard.

Rafe lay with his face in the dirt, his vision fading in and out. He knew he had to get help fast. The longer they had Briana, the farther away they'd get.

But every time he tried to move, his head spun, and he blacked out for a few seconds.

"Can't give up," he muttered. "Bree needs me."

He tried again to roll onto his back. He blacked out only to feel something warm and wet scraping across his skin. When he opened his eyes, Lucy lay beside him, licking his face.

"Hey, I thought you were dead."

She continued licking, whining softly.

This time when Rafe rolled onto his back, he didn't black out. He was able to sit up without falling again. Then he folded his legs beneath him and staggered to his feet, swaying. He thought he'd fall to the ground, but he managed to remain upright long enough to get to the cabin and through the door Briana had left open.

Once inside, he found a knife in the kitchen utensils and fumbled to get it into his hands behind his back. After several failed attempts, he finally sawed through the plastic and freed his wrists. He lunged for the satellite phone and dialed Hank.

"Briana?" Hank answered.

"No. Donovan."

"Fuck," Hank cursed. "They got her, didn't they?"

Rafe had a lot more curses he wanted to say, but they would serve no purpose. "Yes."

"You okay?" Hank asked.

"I will be," Rafe said. "I hope they don't hurt

Briana. I should've been more prepared. They brought more than a dozen men to secure her."

"I've gathered as many of my guys as I could. We're on our way."

The roar of rotor blades echoed off the hillside.

"I have a feeling it's too late. Sounds like they're taking her out by chopper."

"Was she still wearing the necklace I gave her?" Hank asked.

Rafe squeezed his eyes shut against the throbbing in his head. "I think so."

"I'll get Swede monitoring her progress on the computer right away. I have the handheld device. We'll be able to see where she's going and hopefully intercept them."

"God, I hope so. I can't believe they sent so many men to get her. The other two times were one- or two-man jobs," Rafe said.

"*El Chefe* must want Alejandra really bad to send a dozen mercenaries in to retrieve someone who might know where her and the baby are hidden. Seems like overkill."

Rafe cringed. "Let's hope they don't kill her once they discover she has no idea where Alejandra is hidden."

"Are you in any shape to meet me at the high-way?" Hank asked. "Looks like the chopper is headed in the direction of Bozeman."

Rafe fought back waves of nausea and pressed a

hand against the growing lump on the side of his head. He didn't have time to pass out. Briana needed him. "I'll be at the highway when you get there."

He shed his jacket, pulled on a T-shirt, slipped his shoulder holster over his arms and buckled it across his chest. Grabbing his AR15, he stowed it on the back seat of his truck and called to Lucy.

The border collie dragged herself up into the truck and settled in the passenger seat. She hadn't run off when he'd released her leash. She seemed to have bonded with him and Briana in the few short days they'd been together. He was glad the blow she'd sustained hadn't killed her. Briana would've been heartbroken.

Briana...

Sweet Jesus, he'd failed to protect her. Even with the surveillance monitors, he'd let them get past him to her. And she'd willingly stepped out of the cabin to save his sorry ass. She was amazing and courageous. By God, he'd bring her back safely, and then go after the man who'd taken her.

Rafe raced down the mountain road, fishtailing around curves, skidding on gravel. The men in Jeeps were long gone, as was the helicopter in which they'd airlifted Briana.

By the time he reached the highway leading into Eagle Rock in one direction and Bozeman in the other, Hank's truck was slowing to a stop. Two more trucks pulled in behind him, and several men climbed out, carrying rifles or handguns.

Hank left his truck and joined Rafe next to his. "The chopper landed at a private airstrip on a ranch this side of Bozeman. I notified the sheriff, but by the time they got out to the ranch, a small jet had taken off. The helicopter was gone, and the jet was well on its way to wherever they're flying her. I'm in contact with the ATC. They're researching the flight now. So far, they don't have a tail number to allow us to identify the owner. The ranch owner where the landing strip was located is an absentee owner. He flies in once a year during hunting season. He didn't know someone was going to land on his property, and he didn't authorize it."

Rafe's fists clenched. "So, at this point, we have no idea where they're taking her."

"Unfortunately, no."

Rafe's jaw hardened. "I want to talk to Alejandra. It's got to be more than a jilted man wanting his woman and child back. Why is he so desperate to get to her that he'd hire a dozen thugs, mercenaries, a helicopter, and a jet plane to find her? And then to transport another woman back instead... It doesn't make sense."

"If someone stole Sadie away, I'd do everything in my power to get her back. But it bears questioning Alejandra to know what *El Chefe* might do next. I'll have my guys bring her to the ranch. Maybe she can shed some light on why the man is so anxious to get her back that he'd kidnap another woman. In the meantime, you might as well come back to the ranch with me. We can monitor Briana's progress on my computer. If they're heading for an airport, we can call the sheriff or police in that area and have them waiting when they land."

"And if they're headed out of the country?" Rafe asked, cold dread settling like a lead weight in the pit of his belly.

"I can call in all my men and organize a rescue operation. I know someone who owns and operates a large cargo plane who could transport us. I also have contacts in Washington with decision-making power over the Special Operations Command. If push comes to shove, we'll launch an extraction operation to get her out."

He'd heard Hank had connections in high places, but to be able to tap into Spec Ops authority was huge. "You can do that?"

"There are a lot of people who owe me a favor. I can cash in my chips. However, we'll need to have all our ducks in a row and all the intel we can dredge up to plead our case."

"Sounds like it'll take a lot of time."

"Most likely, it won't happen overnight," Hank said, shrugging. "But I think we could mobilize in under forty-eight hours." He frowned at Rafe's truck. "What kills me is how he found you in the first place."

His eyes narrowed. "I'm betting he had a tracker placed on your truck."

Rafe stared at the vehicle in the glare from Hank's headlights. "It's possible. They could have tagged it when they found Briana's cellphone. She'd left it in her purse, locked up in the truck when we stopped for the night in Springfield, Illinois."

"And they waited to attack until you two came out of the hotel." Hank nodded. "It makes sense. Let's leave your truck here. He can find my place easily enough, but why make it easy?" Hank jerked his head toward his men and his truck. "Let's get this ball rolling."

Hank led the way. Rafe climbed into the passenger seat of Hank's truck.

Within the next fifteen minutes, they were rolling through the gates of White Oak Ranch.

Sadie came out on the porch, dressed in jeans and a sweatshirt, her brow furrowed. "I'm so sorry to hear about Briana." She held the door as the men marched into the house and downstairs to the Brotherhood Protectors' HQ-bunker beneath Hank and Sadie's ranch house.

Hank made quick introductions to the men standing around. "You've met Swede." He motioned to a barrel-chested man with brown hair and brown eyes. "Tate Parker, former Delta Force."

Rafe's eyes narrowed. "Don't I know you?"

The man's lips curled upward at the corners. "We

met briefly on a mission in Afghanistan a couple years ago. You might remember me as Bear. That's what people call me."

Rafe nodded. "That's right, Bear Parker. You ran into that building to pull a few kids out after the Taliban lobbed a grenade at it."

Bear nodded, his lips thinning. "Got all but one out alive."

Hank jerked his thumb toward a man with dark hair and darker eyes. "This is Taz Davila, former Army Ranger."

Rafe shook hands with the man.

The next man had black hair and blue eyes. "This is Boomer, or Brandon Rayne, former Navy SEAL," Hank said.

Next was a man with dark hair graying significantly at the temples. "Chuck Johnson is the old man of the team. Prior Navy SEAL."

Taz leaned toward Rafe. "Don't underestimate him. Chuck's in top physical condition and can outrun, outshoot and out-bullshit any of us, any day of the week." He grinned and held up his hands in surrender when Chuck glared at him.

After shaking hands with all the men. Rafe turned to Swede. "Where is she now?"

"They're flying over Colorado right now," Swede reported.

"There has to be a way to intercept that plane."

"It would take too much red tape to scramble

fighter planes to intercept a private jet for a civilian," Hank said. "All we can hope is that they land somewhere in the States, and we can get local law enforcement to seize them."

Rafe paced the room. "We can't just stand around waiting for them to land."

"We're not." Hank glanced up from a simple cellphone. "My guys are on their way now with Alejandra. We can spend the time we're waiting to see where Briana lands by questioning Alejandra."

"By bringing Alejandra here, you're exposing her."

Hank held up the cellphone. "We're using burner phones to communicate, and we're using a van painted like a mail delivery vehicle to get her in and out. I have six guys in the van with her and several positioned at the gate for when they arrive. They're on their way now. Should be here in the next ten minutes."

"Anyone want coffee or something stronger to drink?" Sadie descended the stairs carrying a tray with a carafe of coffee and mugs.

Hank hurried to her, relieved her of her burden and set the tray on the table. "I told you that you don't have to wait on us. Besides, you're not supposed to carry anything heavy," he chastised her. Then he pulled her into his arms and kissed her soundly. "Go back to bed. Emma will be up at dawn, and you'll be exhausted."

"I gave Daphne a heads-up," Boomer said. "She

and Maya can come over and help watch Emma while Sadie catches up on her sleep."

"Thank you, Boomer," Sadie said. "I'd love to see Daphne, and Emma enjoys playing with Maya."

Boomer smiled and ducked his head to send a text to Daphne.

Rafe liked how everyone knew each other. Being the new guy, he felt as though he was still on the outside looking into a tight-knit organization. He knew he'd get over that soon enough, and he sure as hell didn't have time to worry about anything other than getting Briana back safely.

A few minutes later, Swede announced Briana's tracer showed her currently over Texas.

Hank's burner phone pinged. He glanced at a text message coming through. "They're here." He shot a look at Swede. "Let them in the gate."

Swede hit a button on his computer keyboard. "Done."

"Thanks." To Rafe, he said, "I'll be right back." Hank left the bunker, running up the steps two at a time and disappearing through the door at the top.

Sadie followed at a more sedate pace, her hand resting on her swollen belly.

When Hank returned, he escorted a dark-haired woman carrying an infant in her arms. She lifted her chin as she walked into the room full of men. Her gaze swept them, coming to rest on Lucy. "I understand the woman who rescued me off the streets of Chicago has been taken by *El Chefe Diablo*'s men."

Rafe crossed to stand in front of the woman. "She helped you. Now, it's time for you to help her. What is it *El Chefe* wants? Is he upset that you ran with his child?"

Alejandra held her baby close to her chest. "*El Chefe* is not in the least interested in this child," she said. "Except that he would use my baby as insurance."

Rafe's brow twisted. "Insurance?"

"He threatened to kill Bella if I did not cooperate with him."

"Holy hell...what kind of cooperation did he want?"

Alejandra looked toward a blank wall. "I kept the books for his organization. He wants me back to continue to do so. And if I don't come back, he will try to kill me." Her lips curled into a cruel smile. "But I have some insurance of my own."

Hank frowned. "How so?"

"I have an actual book identifying every one of his business partners and what kind of money, services or products have passed between them. There are names in there that could cause major upset in many countries, including the United States. I have hidden that book with an attorney, who has special instructions to mail it to the DEA if I don't call every three days to tell him not to."

Rafe's heart sank to the pit of his belly. Briana was caught up in something even more dangerous than a drug lord wanting his girl and baby back.

"If word gets out that this book exists, there will be a huge uproar in Mexico City, Bogotá, Paris, London and on Capitol Hill in Washington, DC. Major political players could lose their positions, even go to jail. *El Chefe* will do anything to keep that from happening. If that book goes public, he himself will be murdered."

"So, it was never about the child," Rafe stated. "It's all about *El Chefe*'s connections and the trouble you could stir up if that information is revealed."

She ran a hand through her hair, the shadows beneath her eyes a deep purple. "When I first started doing books for the cartel, I was fresh out of college. I'd just returned from university in the United States to my home in El Salvador. I didn't realize I was going to work for a cartel. I thought it was a regular accounting job. The money was good. Better than anywhere else around. I couldn't resist. By the time I figured out what was happening, it was too late. Once you go to work for the cartel, there's only one way out—in a body bag." She smoothed a hand over the baby's shock of dark curls. "Then I had Bella. I realized I couldn't raise her in that environment. I knew *El Chefe* would use her to keep me working for him. He'd threaten to kill her, and carry out that threat, if I tried to leave."

"That's awful." Sadie had joined them in the basement, carrying a sleepy Emma on her hip. "I don't blame you for wanting to escape."

Alejandra gave Sadie a brief nod. "I started documenting all of the clients, partners and connections to the cartel. I noted how much money was involved, what products and services. Once I had all that information, I compiled it into a notebook and mailed it to a lawyer in the States, asking him to hold it without opening it. If I did not call him every three days, he was instructed to mail it to the DEA. I'm due to call today."

"How did you escape?" Rafe asked.

She glanced down at her baby, her face softening. "*El Chefe* didn't know that I wanted to leave. I kept my plans to myself. I had fake passports made. I told him that a good friend of mine from college was dying of cancer, and that she'd asked to see me and Bella before she passed. I told him she lived in Chicago. He allowed me to fly to the States to see her. I kept my cellphone and called when I landed to reassure him I was indeed visiting a friend and would be back soon.

"As soon as I left the plane, I tried to disappear into the city, but he'd arranged to have men follow me. At first, I think to keep me safe. When I noticed I was being followed, I ducked into a shopping center and then into a women's changing room. From there, I made my way through a rear exit. I'd lost them, but I knew they would report back to *El Chefe*. Before they could notify him, I called him to say I had enjoyed a little shopping and was stopping to get something to eat before I joined my friend. I had hoped when his men called, he'd be placated by the fact I'd initiated a call and checked in. I'd hoped it would buy me time to find a safe place to hide. Then it started to rain. That's when I spotted *El Chefe*'s men and ducked into an alley. They passed the alley and kept moving. That's when Briana found us."

Rafe studied her expression, trying to determine whether she was telling the truth. "Briana said she found your phone in her purse after she'd dropped you at the shelter."

Alejandra's cheeks reddened. "When I realized *El Chefe* would eventually figure out that I had not gone to a friend's death bed, I knew he could trace my cell-phone. So I put it into Briana's purse, figuring she would take it away with her. It's my fault he went after her. If she hadn't helped me, she wouldn't be on her way to El Salvador."

"Why would he take Briana when he wanted you?"

Alejandra shrugged. "Apparently, he figured out that Briana helped me. And he knows me. I won't let someone else die because of my defection. He'll offer to make a trade. And when he does, I'll go to El Salvador, so that Briana can come home."

The baby stirred in her mother's arms and whimpered.

Alejandra looked up. "I'll make that trade, but I have one request."

"And what would that be?" Hank asked.

"Please, someone take my baby. Give her a home and the love she needs to flourish. Bella deserves a better life than the one she had with me."

Swede called out. "They stopped in Monterrey, Mexico."

Alejandra nodded. "They'll fuel up there. There's a ranch outside of Monterrey with an airstrip and jet fuel for men who don't want to land their planes at public airports to refuel. *El Chefe*'s shipments stop there when they fly from El Salvador to the US and back. It won't be long before they land, full stop, in El Salvador."

"At this point, everything we know is conjecture," Hank said. "We don't really know what he plans to do with Briana."

Tears glittered in her eyes, but she blinked them away. Her chin lifted. "I guarantee he will try to make a trade. He wants me. He thinks that all this information is in my head," she said, tapping her temple, "and that if I get loose, I can tell whoever wants to know about all of his dealings. Leaking that information could bring a stop to his operations, or make his clients lose their trust in him and want him dead." She held out her hand. "If you have a burner phone,

one that can't be traced, I'll prove to you that this is his plan."

Hank fished in his front pocket for and pulled out a cellphone. He handed it to her. "This is the burner phone I used to communicate with the men who've been guarding you. The number is taped to the back."

Alejandra dialed the international number direct to *El Chefe* and waited. She switched the phone's audio to speaker so that all could hear. Voicemail picked up on the other end. The message was in Spanish. She left a message, also in Spanish. Then, in English, she added, "Call this number." She left the number for the burner phone.

Moments later, the phone buzzed. Alejandra answered using the speaker option.

A man speaking angry Spanish yelled into the speaker.

She spoke to him in a calm, resigned tone.

Rafe only picked up a few of the words she spoke in Spanish, but at one point, he heard her mention "*Señorita* Briana Hayes." He wished he'd paid more attention in high school Spanish class. At the end of the conversation, he picked up the words, *"Estaré ahí pronto."* I will be there soon.

Alejandra ended the call and looked across at Hank.

Hank turned to his man, Taz Davila.

Taz nodded. "It's like she said. He wants to make a

trade. He has Briana, and he's not going to give her up until Alejandra shows up in El Salvador."

Rafe turned to Hank. "So, what are we going to do? I know Briana wouldn't want us to turn over Alejandra to the cartel."

Alejandra shook her head. "It's the only way. He will not let her go, until he has me. If I'm not there in a certain amount of time, he'll start hurting her. Eventually, he'll kill her."

"She's not in El Salvador yet," Hank said. "Let me talk to some of my contacts and see what we can come up with."

Rafe's eyes narrowed. "Sounds like an extraction mission to me."

Alejandra frowned. "What do you mean by contacts?"

"I have some friends in high places who might be able to help us," Hank said.

She shook her head. "Some of the clients and partners on my list are high up on the political chain in the US. If you stir that hornet's nest, I won't be able to get to El Salvador to make the trade. They won't let me live that long."

Hank nodded. "Understood. I'll present it as purely an extraction case of a US citizen. I won't mention that it's a trade."

"*El Chefe* gave me twenty-four hours to get back with him on arrangements for my return to El Salvador. He will expect me there shortly afterward."

"Good," Hank said. "That gives me time to work my connections."

Over the next twenty-four hours, Hank performed miracles. He organized a plane to transport his team of Brotherhood Protectors. He contacted his source in the Special Operations Command and arranged for an extraction mission using Rafe's former Delta Force team out of Fort Hood, Texas. He also contacted the DEA, who had undercover boots on the ground in El Salvador. They would perform reconnaissance of the cartel's stronghold.

Two DEA agents were mobilized quickly and were at the airport when the plane carrying Briana landed. They witnessed a dozen of the cartel's men escorting Briana off the plane then departing in a convoy of vehicles that headed toward *El Chefe's* compound.

Rafe was amazed that by the time the Brotherhood Protectors boarded the plane Hank secured to fly them to El Salvador, that they were fully equipped with weapons, ammunition and protective gear. The items had been stored in crates marked as movie cameras, props and electronics, supposedly destined for a remote location within the country of El Salvador to prepare to film an action-adventure film, starring Sadie McClain.

They remained in close communication with the Delta Force team that had been mobilized and was scheduled to arrive by commercial flight around the same time. They would meet on the ground in the target country and form a formidable team that would be ready, and in place, when Alejandra appeared to make the trade for Briana's freedom at *El Chefe*'s compound.

Rafe hoped all went according to plan, and that they were able to extract both Briana and Alejandra from the cartel leader's clutches without losing either woman or any of the team of Delta Force soldiers.

He understood plans were only good for starting a mission. They rarely executed exactly as intended.

# CHAPTER 10

THE MEN who'd loaded Briana into the Jeep and transported her down the hill to a clearing where a helicopter waited didn't say a word to her. She asked them where they were taking her, but they remained stoically silent, refusing to give her an answer. They secured her wrists with zip-ties, thankfully in front of her, and then strapped her into the helicopter, an armed guard on either side of her.

Thirty minutes later, the helicopter set down on a landing strip on a large ranch where a jet airplane waited. Briana's heart sank into the pit of her belly. She was in for a much longer ride than she'd imagined.

A couple of men speaking Spanish marched her up the steps and onto the jet. At that point, she figured she was on her way to meet the man Alejandra had tried to escape. She was on her way to

El Salvador to answer to *El Chefe Diablo*, the Devil Boss. The only thing that kept her from breaking down into tears was the knowledge that they'd spared Rafe's life. Even if she never saw the United States again, she would know that Rafe was alive and he'd be doing everything in his power to find her and bring her home.

The men who accompanied her on the plane carried military-grade rifles. If she wasn't mistaken, they were AK-47s. Russian-made rifles she'd seen pictures of in news clips from all over the world. They did give her water to drink and allowed her to use the lavatory aboard the plane. It wasn't like she could escape through a window. Not at 35,000 feet in the air. She must have fallen asleep somewhere over Oklahoma or Texas. When they landed to refuel, it was daylight and the signs at the landing strip were in Spanish. She wasn't sure where they were, but she suspected Mexico. The men with the guns didn't allow her to leave the plane, and they were on their way again as soon as the fuel trucks had finished filling the plane's tanks.

By the time they landed at their destination, Briana was bone tired. She'd slept a little, sitting up, but she was worried about Rafe and heartsick for Lucy. The last she'd seen the dog, she'd been lying on the ground after being hit with a club. The pain in Briana's wrists, where the hard plastic of the zip-ties had rubbed the skin raw, seemed inconsequential in comparison to Rafe's and Lucy's suffering. So far, the men who'd kidnapped her hadn't done more than shove her a couple of times. She was sure the Devil Boss had a harsher punishment in store for her once she arrived at his compound.

Dread built with every passing mile they drove away from the airport and into the jungles of El Salvador. If she could, she'd escape, but making her way back to civilization might prove to be difficult and dangerous. She wasn't sure what kinds of animals she might encounter, but they would be preferable to the men of the cartel who had, as Rafe had warned, killed entire families, including women and children, because their boss didn't like the sound of their dogs barking.

Briana had read that cartels were notorious for making examples out of people who crossed them. Sometimes they hung them in their villages or mowed them down at family gatherings. The fact that Briana had assisted Alejandra in her escape and evasion of *El Chefe*'s men made her a prime target for retribution.

By the time they reached the cartel compound, Briana's belly rumbled. She hadn't eaten since the night before, and the heat and humidity of the jungle left her feeling dehydrated. What she wouldn't give for a tall jug of ice water.

The compound consisted of high stucco walls with a heavy wooden gate. Two guards stood on either side, also equipped with AK-47s. When their cavalcade arrived, the guards met the first vehicle, their weapons drawn, ready to fire into the vehicle. Whatever the driver of that vehicle said was enough to convince the guards to stand down and allow the vehicles to enter the compound.

Once inside, Briana studied the layout. If she planned an escape, she'd need to know how many buildings stood between her and the walls and how many guards she'd have to get past to get through the gate or go over the top of the wall. Two guards at the gate, men on the wall behind the gate. A man on the top of the first building closest to the gate with a rifle aimed at the vehicles entering. Her heart sank deeper. She wasn't a trained combatant. She didn't have the skills to fight her way free. But she had a brain and courage. She would figure out how to free herself.

Briana couldn't wait for someone to rescue her. That might never happen. She wasn't an important political figure or a celebrity. The US government didn't send the army to rescue a single female kidnapped from the mountains of Montana. Especially one they'd never heard of. If she wanted to live, she had to get herself out of the compound and to the nearest US consulate or embassy.

First, she had to get the zip-tie off her wrists.

The caravan of black SUVs came to a halt in front

of a palatial stucco house with white columns and curved arches.

Briana half expected the Devil Boss himself to step out of the building to greet his prisoner.

He didn't.

She was dragged out of the SUV and marched into the building, through a wide foyer and down a hallway to a tall wooden door. The guard in front of her knocked and said something in Spanish.

A voice inside barked a response.

The guard opened the door. Her escorts shoved her through and stood beside her in front of a large desk made of ornately carved mahogany. A man with thick black hair and a dark mustache sat behind the desk, his arms crossed over his chest. For a long moment, he stared at Briana, his eyes narrowing.

Finally, he stood and walked over to her. "You are responsible for depriving me of my property."

Briana's brow twisted. "And what property is that?"

"Alejandra Villareal," he said, his lip curling back in a sneer.

Briana lifted her chin. Though she was shaking inside, she refused to let the man see an ounce of fear. "I'm not familiar with how things work in El Salvador, but in the US, slavery has been abolished. People aren't considered property."

He backhanded her, the heavy ring on his finger cutting into Briana's cheek.

Pain shot through her face. She lifted her bound hands to press against the gash his ring had opened on her face. Tears welled automatically in her eyes. Briana blinked, refusing to let even one fall.

The cartel leader glared at her. "You should not have interfered in a matter that did not concern you."

"Helping people in need is always my concern. I would do it all again. Alejandra is not your property."

"You are wrong. Alejandra belongs here," he said, his tone forceful. "Tell me…where is she?"

Briana lifted her chin. "I don't know."

He nodded. "I thought not. We found the women's shelter where you took her outside of Chicago. They said they did not know of a woman and a child meeting Alejandra's description. We searched the building and did not find her."

Thank God. Briana fought the urge to smile. She hoped no one had been injured during the search.

"Alejandra was there. We know from tracking her cellphone. We didn't get there in time. Your friends took her before we arrived. It's funny how people will talk when you threaten their children. The shelter organizer refused to answer our questions, but one of the guests was eager to give us answers when we took her three-year-old daughter."

Briana gasped. "You bastard." Anger burned deep in Briana's gut. If she'd had her .40 caliber pistol on her, she'd have shot this man who would use a child as a pawn in his vicious game.

"When we had all the information they had to give, I had my men burn the shelter to the ground."

Briana sucked in a sharp breath. She felt as if she'd been sucker-punched in the belly. "You are not a man. You're not even an animal. Animals have more compassion than you."

His lips curled in a sneer. "I did not build an empire by being kind to strangers." His brow lowered. "Alejandra *will* return to El Salvador, or she will be responsible for your torture and eventual death."

Briana's gut clenched. Death didn't worry her, as long as it was swift. The idea of being tortured sent shivers of fear throughout her body. She refused to let it consume her. Her mother had always told her and her brother to never borrow trouble. Never fear something that had yet to happen. And in this case, she had to do something to keep it from happening. Briana had to find her way out of this situation before the Devil started down the path of torture.

He said something in Spanish to one of the guards. The guard left the room and returned with a tray of food and drink and set it on a small table near a chair.

The Devil Boss nodded to the tray. "For now, you are my guest. But that will change if Alejandra does not come to her senses and return."

Briana's belly rumbled loudly. She wanted to tell the man where he could shove his food and drink.

She wanted to rebel against anything he wanted her to do. But reason forced her to consider her need for sustenance to help her in her escape. She might have to traipse through the jungle for days without food or water. Better that she consume what she could when offered. She didn't know when her next meal might come.

The Devil Boss spoke again in Spanish. One of the guards pulled a wicked-looking knife out of a scabbard strapped to his leg and came at Briana.

She backed away, running into the guard behind her.

The guard laughed, grabbed her bound wrists and sliced through the zip-tie, scraping her skin with the sharp edge of the blade.

Briana winced. As soon as the plastic tie popped free, she pressed her wrists to her sides to stop the bleeding.

*El Chefe* frowned. "He cut you?"

Briana's chin rose. "It's nothing," she lied, holding her wrist tightly against her jeans.

The Devil Boss grabbed her wrist and yanked it toward him, getting blood on his hands. "*El idiota!*" he shouted and let out string of curses in Spanish. He took the rifle out of the offending guard's hands and spoke angrily in Spanish.

The guard raised his hands and answered, as if pleading.

"Really. It didn't hurt," Briana said.

*El Chefe* pressed the rifle into the man's chest and stared at him through slitted eyes. For a long moment, he held that stance. Then, he said, "Bang."

The guard's eyes widened, and his body tensed. When the gun didn't go off, he let go of the breath he'd been holding in a relieved whoosh.

The Devil Boss spoke softly, *"Pagas por tus errores."* Then he shot the man pointblank.

Briana screamed and staggered backward as the guard's eyes rounded and his mouth opened as if to say something. Then he collapsed to the floor and lay still.

The Devil Boss turned to Briana, pointing the rifle at her chest. "I will translate for you," he said. "You pay for your errors."

Briana sucked in a breath, her heart pounding hard against her chest. She fully expected the cartel leader to shoot her next. She almost welcomed it to end the tumult of fear roiling inside.

Instead, he tossed the rifle to another guard and waved a hand toward the body on the floor. *"Limpia este desastre,"* he said and walked away from Briana.

A couple of his men grabbed the arms and legs of the dead guard and carried him out of the room.

As the cartel leader reached his desk, he turned and jerked his head toward Briana. *"Llévala lejos."*

The remaining guard clasped her arm and dragged her toward the door.

"You might as well let me go," Briana said, her voice shaking. "I don't know where Alejandra is."

"Your friends know where to find her. If they want you to come home alive, they will bring Alejandra to me." The phone on his desk rang, and a smile curled his lip. "I suspect this will be Alejandra now. She called earlier. She knows what is at stake. Now, it's only a matter of time as to when she will return to her country. When she does, we might decide to let you go." He shrugged. "Or maybe, we will keep you and sell you to the highest bidder or use you as an example to others who might interfere in our operations." He waved his hand.

The guard dragged her toward the door.

The cartel leader let the phone ring a few more times, tapping his fingers on the desktop, as if letting Alejandra stew.

As her captor escorted her out of *El Chefe*'s study, Briana heard the man talking. She couldn't make out the words and wouldn't have been able to translate, anyway.

If it was Alejandra, it meant Hank had been successful in moving her to Montana. It also meant that all Briana had done to protect the woman and her baby was for naught. Thankfully, Hank's men had moved her before the Devil Boss's men had arrived at the shelter.

She hoped Alejandra would refuse to make the

trade. The woman's baby needed her more than Briana needed to live.

At the same time, Briana worried about the forms of torture the cartel leader would inflict on her to force Alejandra to comply. Could she withstand the pain?

The guard took her to a room at the end of a long hallway, unlocked the door and shoved her inside. As soon as he released his hold on her arm, Briana spun and darted around the guard. She almost made it past him when he grabbed her hair and yanked her backward.

Briana fell, landing hard on her ass.

Instead of letting her rise to her feet, the guard dragged her by the hair into the room, stepped back, pointing his rifle at her chest and backed through the doorway.

Scrambling to her feet, Briana ran for the door. It shut before she reached it. The metal click of a key being turned in the lock let her know she was well and truly stuck in the dark prison. With no windows and no lamps or light fixtures, she had to wait for her eyes to adjust to the darkness. The only thing saving her from pitch blackness was the sliver of light coming from beneath the wooden door.

Briana closed her eyes and willed her vision to adjust quickly. The sooner she could see, the sooner she could inspect her prison for possible ways to escape.

When she opened her eyes again, she looked around at the dim interior of a small, square room. In one corner was a toilet and a sink. In the other was a cot, bare of pillows or blankets. Not that she needed blankets in the heat of the El Salvadoran jungle. She tested the sink. The water appeared to be clear and fresh. She washed her face and hands, careful not to ingest any for fear of parasites. Eventually, she'd have to have water, but for now, she preferred to do without.

Footsteps sounded on the Saltillo tile outside the door of her prison, and the metal lock clicked.

The guard who'd brought her there pointed his rifle at her and said something in Spanish she assumed translated to "Stay where you are, or I'll shoot your ass." Another guard brought the tray of food she'd left in the study into the room and set it on the bed. Then he backed out, the door closed, and the lock sealed her inside.

The tray contained a small round pancake-looking things that appeared to be thick flour tortillas.

Briana lifted one, sniffed and tested a bite, only to find the interior filled with refried beans. It tasted all right and wasn't too spicy. She ate all of one and started into another. On the tray was also a plastic bottle of water. Trusting it only slightly more than the water out of the tap, she sipped it, trying to quench her thirst. The humidity and the close confines of the room already had her sweating. She'd need the water to keep from dehydrating. After she'd finished two of the small, stuffed pancakes, she fit one into her pocket to hold in case she managed an escape.

Another careful study of the room helped her to identify items she might use for weapons. If she could knock out a guard, she might sneak past him to get out of the main house. The challenge would then be getting out of the compound. The wall was too high for her to scale without help. If she could find a ladder or something to help her get over the top, she'd need to climb over away from the main gate and hope there weren't guards posted all around the perimeter. She just needed a chance, and she'd make the best of it. The jungle looked pretty tame compared to the kind of justice *El Chefe Diablo* dished out. Briana needed to figure a way out. The sooner the better. Then Alejandra wouldn't have to risk her newfound freedom to get Briana out of a tight situation.

There had to be a way.

Briana went to work pulling and tugging at the legs of the bed. The metal was firm and needed a screwdriver and a wrench to dismantle the frame. The plumbing was bare bones. She might have used the lid to the toilet, if it had one. The tank was one that was mounted high on the wall with a string to pull for flushing. She might be able to use the string to stretch across the door to trip or confuse the guards. Filing that thought away, she skimmed her hands along the walls, searching for any holes or soft spots she could dig out to carve an exit through the wall. The wall was smooth. Tapping her knuckles against it, she realized it was probably made of concrete blocks. Without a chisel and several weeks of painstaking work, she wouldn't make much of a dent in the structure.

If she wanted out of that room, she had to leave through the door. Unless the guard got careless, she doubted an opportunity would present itself. What guard wanted to face *El Chefe Diablo* after losing a prisoner? Especially after one of the guards was murdered for scraping Briana's wrists with his knife.

An hour passed. Two guards showed up to escort her back down the long hallway to the cartel leader's study.

"Give them proof of life. Talk to the camera." He nodded toward a man who held a smart phone.

This was her chance to get her message across, not fight the monster who held her hostage. Briana stared at the smartphone camera, her head held high. "Alejandra, if you get this message, don't come to El Salvador. Seek asylum from the US government, stay in the States and raise your baby."

*El Chefe* cursed and started toward her.

Briana continued, talking faster, "You were right

to leave this monster. Stay away. Don't worry about me. I don't have a child. You do."

The Devil Boss grabbed her hair and yanked back her head. He stuck a wicked, long knife up to her throat and spoke to the phone. "If you want her to live another day, you'll be on a plane in the next twelve hours. After that, I will start taking her apart, one piece at a time, starting with her pretty ear." He touched the tip of the knife to Briana's ear and pricked it, drawing blood.

Briana bit down hard on her lip to keep from crying out.

"Twelve hours." *El Chefe* lowered the knife, released his grip on her hair and backhanded her hard enough that she flew across the room and landed on her hands and knees.

He made a cutting motion across his throat. The man holding the smart phone stopped the video and handed the phone to his boss. He pressed a few buttons, keyed a message and pressed send.

"Now, we will see if your life is worth anything," *El Chefe* said, motioning to the guard. "*Llévala lejos.*"

The guard jerked her to her feet, walked her out of the room and back down the long hallway to her prison.

Still dizzy from being hit in the face, Briana could barely keep up with the man. He half-walked, half-dragged her until they reached the room. Then he shoved her inside and slammed the door shut.

Briana stumbled and fell to the floor, the same cheek he'd cut the first time bleeding again. She lay there for a few minutes, praying Alejandra did as she'd said and stayed in the US. If she came home, she would have no freedom and live in constant fear for her life and for that of her little girl.

Briana understood what it meant for her if Alejandra didn't come, and she prayed that if she couldn't find a way out, that she'd die sooner rather than later.

# CHAPTER 11

Thirty-six hours after Briana's abduction, the plane greased the landing and came to a halt in San Salvador, the capital of El Salvador. They couldn't get there fast enough for Rafe. After seeing Briana bleeding at the hand of *El Chefe,* Rafe was ready for a fight. Being cooped up on a plane for hours, did little to reduce his anger.

He was glad to be on the ground again. They hadn't saved Briana yet, but at least he was in the same country as the pretty social worker and had more of a chance of saving her than when they were back in Montana.

Hank had tapped on one of his movie star wife's friends who owned a large plane they used to transport movie-making equipment and personnel to foreign locations. They'd loaded the cargo hold with everything they'd need to mount an operation to extract Briana from the clutches of one of the most notorious cartel leaders in Central America.

The plane parked in the general aviation side of the airport and was met by the customs officials of the country. Hank had arranged for them to see a crate full of movie equipment. After they'd checked the crate, they allowed the team to load the crates into waiting trucks inside a hangar.

A bus arrived from the commercial side of the international airport, and the Delta Force team from Fort Hood joined them.

Rafe had never been happier to see his old team as he was that day.

"Dude, I send you to protect my sister, and this is how you treat her?" Ryan "Dash" Hayes pulled Rafe into a bear hug. When he leaned back, he frowned, staring at the blood on his hand. "Get in a fight with one of those Montana grizzlies?"

"A grizzly would have been easier to deal with." Hope built in Rafe's chest. With his team there, they had half a chance against an army of cartel thugs. "I wasn't sure they'd send you guys. I thought you were on a mission."

"We were on the way back when I got the call from Bree," Dash said. "I didn't realize just how bad it was."

"Neither did we. Obviously. *El Chefe* sent in a dozen of his mercenaries to get her out, along with a chopper and plane."

"We heard. You're lucky to be alive from what Hank told us." Hayes tipped his head to the others standing behind him. "The guys are all glad to see you. We're hoping we can talk you into re-enlisting. It's not the same without our token Irishman." He stepped aside.

"Yeah, man. I don't have anyone to nag me to clean my weapon or change my socks on mission," Doug "Dog" Masters said. He hugged Rafe then punched him in the arm. "You need to come back."

"No shit." Craig Bullington, otherwise known as Bull, pulled Rafe into a bone-crunching hug. The big mountain of a man could bench press four hundred pounds without breaking a sweat. "We miss having you around."

"Speak for yourself." Mike "Blade" Calhoun clasped forearms with Rafe. "Now, I have half a chance with the ladies without Donovan around to steal them. Unless he's found one of his own. Then he can come back."

Dash frowned. "You ain't been hitting on my sister, have you?"

"Dash, I hope your sister is better looking than you," Sean "Mac" McDaniel said, pushing him aside to get close to Rafe to hug him. "*Is* she better looking than Dash?"

"Much better," Rafe said. "And she's amazing, kind and selfless. Unlike her brother."

Dash's eyes narrowed. "You didn't answer my question. You been hitting on Bree?"

"If he has, he's smart enough not to tell you," John "Tank" Sanders, the old man of the team, said. He shook Rafe's hand. "Good to see you."

"Great to see you, Tank. You ever buy that piece of property out by Copperas Cove?" Rafe asked.

Tank nodded. "Closed on it the day before we shipped out on our last mission. Haven't had a chance to get out there and see what needs to be done. Hope to build a house out there, someday."

"Are you the next man to bail on the team?" Rafe asked. "You should be getting close to your twenty-year mark."

"I have three more years to go," Tank said.

"Tank, you should see about getting a desk job," Rucker Sloan said, reaching in to shake Rafe's hand. "You're getting too old for Delta Force. Or maybe, we all need to be like Donovan and bail before we're too old."

"Shut the fuck up," Tank said. "I'm not old. I can still outrun, outshoot and outfight any one of you dumbasses."

Mac clapped a hand on Tank's shoulder. "A little sensitive, are we?"

"It's good to see you all," Rafe said. "I didn't realize just how much I missed you bunch of jerks."

"Yeah, you'll be back," Bull predicted.

Rafe shook his head. "Nah. Montana is pretty amazing."

"Montana? Or my sister?" Dash's eyes narrowed.

Rafe's jaw hardened. "We're getting your sister back. I shouldn't have let them get to her."

Hank joined them. "You were far outnumbered. I should have provided more support."

"We had no idea he would send so many or launch such an elaborate attack to capture Briana. He wanted Alejandra. Still does."

"It's how he operates." Alejandra approached the group of Delta Force men. "If he can't get what he wants directly, he makes certain he can negotiate for what he wants. He just has to get the right carrot to dangle." Alejandra touched Rafe's arm. "You couldn't have known. I shouldn't have taken up Briana on her offer to find me and my Bella refuge. She would never have been a target if I'd just moved on my own."

"We can stand around swapping regrets all day, but we're better off getting to the compound," Hank said. "The undercover DEA agents have agreed to meet with us in a conference room inside this hanger to pass on what information they were able to gather. Let's get this operation underway."

The team moved into the conference room, where they met with the two agents who'd been as close as they could get to *El Chefe*'s compound in the jungle. They'd counted as many as thirty of the cartel leader's men coming and going from that location. Since they'd taken Briana into the compound, she hadn't come back out, that much they knew.

They'd been covering *El Chefe*'s movements for some time now, gathering information about his contacts, clients and partners.

Hank had briefed his team of Brotherhood Protectors on the way to El Salvador. They weren't to mention anything about the book Alejandra had with all that information. He didn't want anyone in El Salvador to know of its existence for fear Alejandra wouldn't make it to the compound to trade for Briana.

The Deltas and the DEA didn't need to know about the book. That was information best kept for another day.

"We have to assume *El Chefe* has people watching us already," Hank said. "Hopefully, he hasn't seen just how many people we brought with us. He'll expect my team to bring Alejandra to the compound. Before that, we need the Deltas in place for backup and to provide cover for when Alejandra makes the trade. We can't let them keep Briana."

"How do we know she's still alive?" Rafe asked, though he hated the thought that she might be otherwise.

At that moment, Hank's burner phone buzzed. He pulled the phone from his pocket. "*El Chefe* just texted a video." He brought the video up on the phone, and they waited while it buffered.

Rafe leaned in and gasped when Briana's image came onto the screen.

"Alejandra, if you get this message, don't come to El Salvador," Briana said. "Seek asylum from the US government, stay in the States and raise your baby."

Briana continued, talking faster, "You were right to leave this monster. Stay away. Don't worry about me. I don't have a child. You do."

*El Chefe* grabbed her hair and yanked her head back. He stuck knife to her throat and looked straight at them. "If you want her to live another day, you'll be on a plane in the next twelve hours. After that, I will start taking her apart, one piece at a time, starting with her pretty ear." He touched the tip of the knife to Briana's ear and pricked it, drawing blood.

Rafe's fists clenched, rage rising in his chest.

"Twelve hours," the cartel leader repeated. The time stamp on the message was from six hours earlier.

That gave them six hours to contact *El Chefe* to arrange the trade. Six hours to get the Deltas in place to support them.

The DEA guys had a hand-drawn diagram of the exterior of the compound and the likely locations of guards posted outside. They'd pulled a satellite image that gave a birds-eye view of the buildings within the compound. The main building appeared to be a large white house, and there were barracks-like buildings at the rear of the walled compound. Several smaller buildings were on either side, possibly for storage. Jungle surrounded the compound on all sides with a gravel road leading in. The trade would have to be made somewhere along the gravel road.

"We don't send Alejandra in until they send Briana out," Rafe said.

"The trade has to be made outside the compound," Hank agreed. "To have any chance of bringing both women back, we need them to be where we can see them. If they get Alejandra inside the compound, it'll complicate her extraction."

"Don't worry about me," Alejandra said. "We need to get Briana out alive. If I go in, take Briana and get the hell out of El Salvador. *El Chefe* cannot be trusted."

"The compound is two hours out of the city," one of the DEA agents said. "You need time to get there and get in place. We've arranged for a couple of produce trucks to get your advance team to within a couple of miles of the compound. They'll go in on foot from there."

The Delta Force team gathered their weapons, protective gear and communications equipment then loaded their duffle bags into the back of the truck. They wore civilian clothing, having agreed that arriving in uniform would alert the cartel to their presence sooner than they wanted.

One of the agents made a call, and minutes later,

trucks pulled into the hangar loaded with boxes of produce arranged so that the soldiers could climb into the back, hunker down amid the boxes and not be seen from the road.

"Great. Let's get this party started," Hank said. "I have a wife and little girl waiting for me back home."

"And I have a baby girl I hope to see again," Alejandra said.

"If all goes according to plan, you should see your daughter soon," Hank said.

*If.*

Rafe prayed the operation that night went according to the plan. At the very least, he hoped they got Briana and Alejandra out alive. Trading one woman for another didn't sit well with him. He preferred to go in with just the team and duke it out. Having the ladies in the line of fire made it trickier and more dangerous.

After his week in the mountains with Briana, Rafe didn't want their time together to end so soon. He liked her a lot and could be well on his way to loving her. Rafe wanted more time with Briana to get to know her even more. At the end of the day, he hoped they'd have that chance.

Briana spent the day working on the legs on the bed, trying to break a leg free. The metal didn't bend, and the screws were in tight, holding the legs to the frame. She needed a screwdriver and a wrench to free the bolts holding it together. Since she had neither of those two items, she moved on to the other items in the room. The bed had no sheets or blankets she could use to throw over the guard. The toilet had no lid she could use to hit the guard with, but the food tray was made of metal. If she could get the guard far enough inside the room, she could hit him with the tray and make her escape.

Getting the guard to open the door would be the first challenge.

Briana stood to the side of the door holding the empty tray. She moaned loudly. "I'm sick. Please, get me a doctor. I'm so sick." She moaned again.

When the door didn't open, she pounded the wooden panel with her fist. "Please, I'm sick and need help. *Por favor.*" She stopped and dropped to the ground with as loud a thump as she could manage and not hurt herself. As soon as she hit the floor, she quietly crawled to the side of the door, lifted the tray and stood, ready for when the guard might finally open the door to check on her.

She waited silently.

And waited.

Just when she thought the guard might not even be on the other side of the door, the lock clicked.

Briana's pulse quickened as she raised the tray over one shoulder, her arms cocked and ready.

A guard pushed open the door with the barrel of his AK-47 and looked inside.

Because it was so dark in the room, he had to push the door wider to let in some light.

Holding her breath, Briana waited for the man to cross the threshold.

When he didn't see her in the triangle of light shining across the floor, he stepped into the room.

Briana swung the tray as hard as she could, slamming it into the man's face.

The man released his hold on the AK-47. It clattered to the hard tiles.

Briana would've dived for the weapon, but the big guard dropped to his knees, landing on the gun. Instead, she hit him on the back of the head and leaped over his shoulder, landing in the hallway. She ran as fast as she could, aiming for the only door she knew led out of the building.

When a man stepped into view in the grand foyer ahead, Briana ducked into an open door that led into a sitting room with dark wood tables and brightly colored sofas. French doors on the other side of the room lured her to the outside light. She ran across the room and had just reached for the door handles when a shout rang out in the hallway.

Grabbing the handles, she yanked open the French doors and ran out into a garden. Unfortunately, the garden was a courtyard, surrounded by four walls. Each had French doors leading onto the garden, but which one would bring her closest to exiting the house? She ran to the door directly across from the one she'd just passed through. More shouts echoed throughout the huge house. If she hoped to escape, she had to do it soon. The door on the opposite side led into a bedroom with a solid wood, four-poster bed with a white eyelet lace comforter that seemed incongruous for a drug lord known for killing.

Footsteps clattered on the paving stones in the garden behind her. Briana dropped to her belly and rolled beneath the bed, wishing she'd had time to close the garden door. Alas, someone was running toward her, giving her no time to hide anywhere but beneath the bed.

She moved to the center, praying whoever it was would run straight through the room to the other side, searching for her. That might give her time to find another way out.

Booted feet entered the room and ran for the door as Briana had hoped. The door opened, but the boots didn't pass through it.

Briana couldn't see what he was doing but guessed he was peering out into the hallway. He called out in Spanish to someone passing by. That person responded, and the man stepped out into the corridor.

Briana held her breath, waiting for the man to leave the room. With the house in an uproar to find her, she knew she wouldn't make it out of the compound without being captured. The thought depressed her, but she wouldn't give up. This was her first attempt. She would try again.

Easing out from under the bed, she crawled out the open French door into the garden and sat on a bench beneath a tree and pulled in a deep breath. She stared at a bird bath, waiting for the guards to find her and return her to her prison.

Footsteps on the paving stones made her stiffen. She wouldn't fight this time. Not with all the cartel's minions searching for her. But she was prepared to duck if one of them decided to take a swing at her.

"You've upset my staff," a voice said behind her.

Briana didn't turn toward *El Chefe*. "You have a lovely garden," she said.

"I like to come out here to read when I want peace and quiet," he said, walking around to stand in front of her. "You know, you can't escape."

"So you say."

"Even if you'd gotten out of the house, you wouldn't have made it past the wall."

"You could be right," she said. "Then again, no one likes to be held prisoner. Some are just more determined than others to be free."

He stared at her, eyes narrowing. "Are you talking about yourself or Alejandra."

Briana pushed to her feet. "You are not a king or a

god. You cannot control the lives of others with your money."

He dipped his head. "No, but I can control them with my army and the mercenaries my money can buy."

"And does it make you happy?" Briana stood in front of the Devil Boss, her shoulders back, her face set in grim lines. "Are you happy controlling other people? Don't you wonder if it's all worth it?"

He spread his arms wide. "I have all this."

"Things," she pointed out. "You have things. What about love and kindness? The people in your life should be what make you happy, not the things. Things don't have feelings."

He snorted. "Things don't stab you in the back or steal from you."

"Is that what happened to you? Did someone you cared about turn on you? Was it Alejandra?"

"No!" he shouted. "It was not Alejandra. She is but an employee, who knows too much about my business to let go. You know nothing about me. And you never will." He looked past her shoulder and said something in Spanish.

Two guards appeared. One had blood drying beneath his nose and a bruise on his cheek. They gripped her arms and half-carried her back to her cell. The food tray had been removed. There was nothing else in the room she could use as a weapon. Her heart sank into her shoes.

Briana could have wallowed in her despair and let loose the tears waiting to fall, but the thought of maybe seeing Rafe again kept her going. They'd had so little time together. She liked him. A lot. She could even see herself falling in love with the man—if given the chance.

The next time the door opened, she'd have to be ready to throat punch the guard and make sure he didn't yell for help as soon as she ran.

If she got another chance, she'd take it.

# CHAPTER 12

WITH BROTHERHOOD PROTECTORS HANK, Swede, Boomer, Taz, Chuck and Bear by his side, and his old Delta Force team supposedly in place around the compound, Rafe dared to hope all could go well once they arrived with Alejandra to make the trade. They didn't try to sneak in like the Delta Force team. Their job was to be there for the trade. The Deltas were there to cover their sixes and make sure *El Chefe* didn't try to take them all out and keep both females.

Hank's men gave the Delta Force team plenty of time to get to their positions and for the sun to sink into the horizon. Two hours out from the designated time, Hank handed Alejandra the burner phone to make her call to the Devil Boss.

She set the audio on speaker and spoke in Spanish, repeating her words in English. "I'll be there in two hours. We will make the trade outside your compound. We will see that *Señorita* Hayes is well and uninjured before I step out of the vehicle. Understood?"

"*Si*. We will have bullets reserved for Miss Hayes if anything goes wrong during the transfer. Understood?"

Rafe's lip curled back in a snarl. He personally wanted to kill *El Chefe* with his bare hands. To watch him choke to death slowly. How a man could torture and kill innocent people on a whim was beyond Rafe's comprehension. Men like the cartel leader needed to be eliminated from society completely.

After Alejandra made the call, they loaded the team into three SUVs then lined up for the drive out to the compound. Taz, Chuck and Boomer took the lead. Hank, Alejandra and Rafe rode in the middle vehicle. Swede and Bear brought up the rear. The Brotherhood Protectors were fully equipped for combat, wearing bullet proof vests, helmets with radios, rifles, handguns, grenades and night vision goggles.

The Delta Team would be in place with a sniper on either side of the entrance, ready to pick off anyone who might try to take out Hank and his team.

They drove in silence to within a mile of the coordinates the DEA agents had given them and slowed to a stop, where they performed a communi-cations check with the Delta Force team. Once everyone was accounted for, the procession continued on to the turnoff. The sun was well on its way toward the horizon, casting the surrounding jungle into deep shadows.

The closer they got to the compound, the faster Rafe's heart beat. He wanted to see Briana, to know for sure she was alive and well. And he wanted to kill *El Chefe* for taking and hurting her. The woman only wanted to do right by people, to ease their suffering. She'd helped Alejandra because she couldn't stand to see a woman and her child exposed to the elements and afraid to seek assistance lest she draw attention to herself and be discovered by the man she'd escaped.

Briana had a big heart and courage like no other woman he knew. Yes, he could be falling in love with her and, for the first time in his life, he was okay with that. He wasn't tempted to return to the Delta Force teams. He realized he wanted a life outside constant deployments to war-torn nations where he could be shot at, blown up or tortured if caught. No, he wanted more in life. He wanted someone like Briana to come home to at night, to explore the mountains with and maybe raise children of their own. Not *like* Briana. He wanted Briana.

As they came to a halt fifty yards from the compound's gate, the lead vehicle stopped, and the men climbed out, standing with their doors open, providing a little protection from potential gunfire.

The gate opened, and several of *El Chefe's* men emerged.

Rafe held his breath, waiting for the most important person to come out of the compound. When she did, he let go of the breath and tightened his hand on his rifle.

Briana stood between two large men, each holding one of her arms. Behind her stood a man with black hair and a black mustache, wearing a white guayabera shirt and dark trousers. He stood with his arms crossed over his chest, his eyes narrowed, surrounded by his men who would take bullets to protect him should anyone decide to start shooting.

Alejandra squared her shoulders, her face pale beneath her naturally dark complexion. "It's time." She leaned close to Hank. "Thank you for helping me. If this plan does not work out, promise to take care of my child. She needs a good home and the love of a family."

"We're going to get you out of this," Hank said.

Alejandra stared hard into his eyes. "Promise."

Hank nodded.

Alejandra turned to Rafe. "I will do my best to make sure your woman gets out alive. Be ready to grab her and get her out of El Salvador. *El Chefe* does not forgive or forget when someone crosses him. If he lives through this, he will seek his revenge."

"Our goal today is to get you and Briana out of here alive," he said.

She cupped his cheek and gave him a gentle smile. "You love her, don't you?"

He nodded without realizing it.

"In some ways, you are like him." She jerked her head toward the compound. "You care enough to go after her."

Rafe frowned. He never wanted to be compared to the cartel leader.

Alejandra raised a hand. "The difference is, you would let her go, if that was what she wanted."

He wouldn't like it, but he couldn't keep someone who wasn't his.

Hank got out of the driver's seat and opened the back door. Rafe got out of the back seat and held out his hand to Alejandra.

She took it and let him help her out. Once her feet were on the ground, she leaned up on her toes and kissed his cheek. "Thank you for coming with me." Then as she stepped away, she plucked one of his grenades off his vest and smiled. "Be ready."

"What the—" Rafe took a step after the woman.

Hank caught his arm. "Let her. She has a plan. We need to be ready."

He glared at Hank. "You knew?"

He tightened his jaw and nodded.

"What if it goes off when she's near Briana?"

"She knows how to use it."

Rafe shook his head. "It's too dangerous."

Alejandra called out in Spanish, and then in English. "Let her go. We meet halfway. Alone."

The Devil Boss said something to his two men.

They released their hold on Briana and stepped back, forming a wall between *El Chefe* and the Americans.

Hank and Rafe passed the other Brotherhood Protectors standing behind the doors of the front vehicle and stood ready to help in whatever way they could.

Alejandra and Briana walked toward each other.

Rafe prayed the cartel men didn't see the grenade or they might shoot her before she got close enough to make the grenade count. If she'd already pulled the pin and they shot her, the grenade could kill both women.

Rafe's muscles bunched. He'd be ready to run in and grab Briana as soon as she got close enough.

God, he didn't like this. His breath caught and held in his lungs as the scene played out in front of him in excruciatingly slow motion.

He'd been involved in a lot of high-risk, high body-count battles, but this one had him the most on edge because he had very little control over what might happen. All he could do was be ready to respond and hope the Deltas were in good positions to pick off the cartel members before they could pick off Briana and Alejandra.

. . .

BRIANA HAD SPENT the afternoon pacing in her prison. Time dragged so slowly she thought she might go crazy. She even did pushups and sit-ups to keep fit while confined. If she stayed much longer, she considered making marks on the wall to count the days.

She'd finally laid on the cot and closed her eyes, hoping to fall asleep so that time would seem to pass quicker. Sleep wouldn't come. Not long after she laid down, the key clicked in the lock, and two guards appeared, glaring at her as if daring her to try something.

They took her by her arms and propelled her down the long hallway to the front entrance and out into the yard of the compound.

Briana looked around, wondering if she could break free of the big men and make a run for it. Or was this what the Devil Boss had been after all along...the trade?

Hell. Briana hoped it wasn't a trade. Alejandra needed to be with her baby, not this lunatic. He would make their lives miserable and possibly end them without a second thought. Because she'd made a run for it, he might even torture her before he killed her.

Torture.

Was the Devil Boss about to perform his first act

of torture on her? Would he record it and send it to Hank and Rafe to make them convince Alejandra to make the trade?

All these thoughts raced through Briana's head in seconds. Then they were at the gate, and the cartel leader was there as well.

As soon as the gate opened and the path cleared of cartel men, Briana could see three SUVs standing at the end of the drive. The lead one stood open and men were outside the vehicles, using the doors as shields.

Briana's heart skipped several beats. She couldn't help but think that shit was about to get real in El Salvador.

Then Hank Patterson got out of the second vehicle and opened the back door.

Rafe emerged.

Briana gasped, and her heart fluttered. He was there. He'd come for her. Her eyes welled with tears she quickly blinked back. The two guards at her side walked her forward a couple of steps and stopped, still holding tightly to her arms.

After Rafe got out of the SUV, he turned and extended his hand.

Alejandra emerged, leaned up and kissed Rafe's cheek.

A short stab of something hit Briana square in the gut. Jealousy? No, the kiss had been quick, as if in thanks. Envy. Probably. She wished she could kiss Rafe's cheek and lips and hold him close.

Then Alejandra called out in Spanish and then English. "Let her go. We meet halfway. Alone."

Her heart pounding, Briana nearly collapsed, when upon a command from their leader, the cartel guards released her arms. She was free but had to walk the gauntlet of the road leading into the compound.

Alejandra stepped away from Hank and Rafe, walked around the open doors of the lead vehicle and kept coming.

"Go," *El Chefe* barked.

Briana lurched forward, rubbing her arms where the men had held her so tightly there would be bruises. The fifty or so yards to the SUVs seemed like a lot more.

As Alejandra neared, it dawned on Briana that she didn't have her baby with her. Where was Bella? The men behind her didn't seem to have her. Was she in one of the vehicles? Her heart stopped for several beats. Had she left Bella in the States?

Her heart squeezed hard in her chest. This woman was sacrificing herself to save Briana. Leaving her baby in the hands of others...

Oh, her heart hurt.

As she approached Alejandra, she shook her head. "You shouldn't have come. Where's Bella?"

"I had to. She's with Sadie. Be ready to run."

Briana frowned. "What?"

Alejandra glanced down at her hand, holding something green with a handle clutched against it. "Just run," Alejandra said as she continued to walk toward the compound.

As the item registered in Briana's mind, she picked up her pace, walking faster. Holy shit. Alejandra had a grenade.

*Dear Lord, please don't let her martyr herself for me.*

Briana glanced over her shoulder as Alejandra approached the phalanx of men surrounding *El Chefe.* In an underhanded toss, she rolled the grenade between the legs of the men guarding the cartel leader. They scrambled, dancing away from the object.

Alejandra spun and ran toward Briana. "Run!" she yelled.

Briana stumbled over her own feet then righted herself and ran as fast as she could.

Alejandra caught up with her, took her arm and pulled her along with her.

An explosion rocked the ground beneath their feet, the force at their backs pushing them forward so fast, they fell to their knees.

Gunfire exploded all around.

"Stay down," Hank called out.

"Cover me!" Rafe cried and ran toward them, hunkered down.

Briana crawled on all fours toward him.

Alejandra did the same, moving as fast as she could.

When Rafe reached them, he pointed to the ground in front of Alejandra. "Stay flat on your belly. I'll be right back."

Alejandra dropped to her belly.

Rafe bent, helped Briana to her feet and, shielding her body, ran her toward the vehicles. As soon as he had her safely behind the bulk of an SUV, he left her and went back for Alejandra.

Briana watched from the relative safety of the SUV as Rafe started to run toward the other woman.

Hank caught him before he got too far. "Cover me."

The founder of the Brotherhood Protectors ran across the open ground, dropping down beside Alejandra.

Briana held her breath, praying Hank and Alejandra made it back to safety, alive.

Hank wrapped his arm around Alejandra, effectively shielding her body with his as he ran with her to the waiting SUVs. He helped her into the back seat of the middle vehicle and slid in beside her. One of his men took the driver's seat.

Rafe returned to Briana and ran with her to the last vehicle, the one closest to the main road. As they reached it, Briana heard the thunder of rotor blades beating the air. She looked up to see a helicopter rising above the canopy of trees.

She turned to Rafe. "Did *El Chefe* get away?"

Rafe's jaw was so tight it twitched as he helped her into the backseat. "I don't know for sure, but he jumped behind the gate and slammed it shut before the grenade exploded."

Briana cursed as she slid across the seat. "That man doesn't deserve to live. He's a monster."

Rafe slipped in beside her and pulled her into his arms.

Swede and Bear climbed into the front seats and closed their doors. Bear spun the vehicle around and raced for the main road heading back to San Salvador, followed by the SUV carrying Hank and Alejandra and the last vehicle with two more of Hank's men.

Rafe spoke into the mic on his helmet's radio. "I have Briana in the lead vehicle." He listened. "That's what I thought. This isn't over as long as *El Chefe* is still alive." He looked across at Briana. "He got away."

"Son of a bitch," Briana said.

He took her hand and held it in his. "The good news is that all of the Delta Force team members got away without injury."

Briana raised his hand to her lips and pressed a kiss to the backs of his knuckles. "Thank you for finding me."

"I wouldn't have stopped looking until I did." He brought her hand to his lips and kissed the tips of her fingers.

"Did you know Alejandra was going to throw a grenade?"

"Not until she stole one from me at the last minute."

Briana cocked an eyebrow. "When she kissed you?"

He grinned. "You saw that?"

Her brows formed a V over her nose. "I did."

"Were you jealous?"

She sighed, her brow smoothing. "Truthfully, I was, a little." Briana leaned her head against his shoulder. "I thought we had a connection up there in the Crazy Mountains, unless it was all one-sided...?" She glanced up at him from beneath her eyelashes.

"If by one-sided, you mean, all on my side, that could be. Because, you see, I have no idea where I stand with you, Briana Hayes. When you left, I felt we had just gotten started. I was falling for you. Now, we've all been traumatized, and we're likely to think we're in love when we're just getting to know each other."

"Why not accept the fact we're in love?" Briana asked. "Life's short, and none of us get out of it alive. Unfortunately, some sooner than others."

He nodded. "You have a point." He leaned close and kissed her lips. "Lucy and I missed you."

"Oh my God, Lucy! She made it?" Briana smiled, her heart swelling. "I thought that bastard killed her when he hit her with the club."

"She made it. I'm sure she's got a headache."

Briana reached up to unbuckle his helmet and pull it off. Then she touched the bruise and knot at his temple. "You should have seen a doctor."

"I'm okay."

She leaned up and pressed a gentle kiss to his injury.

"You're the one I'm worried about." He brushed the backs of his knuckles below the gash on her cheek. "Who did this?"

Her eyes narrowed. "The Devil Boss. I'm glad we got Alejandra out of there. She doesn't deserve to live in that kind of fear. The man is horrible." She shivered, remembering how he'd toyed with the guard who'd cut her before killing him.

She lay her cheek on Rafe's shoulder. "I'm worried."

"You're out of there."

"I know. But *El Chefe* is still alive. He won't let this slide. He'll be back for more. I'll be surprised if we make it out of El Salvador without further backlash from him."

"The Deltas will be right behind us. They'll make sure we aren't tailed by the cartel men. The DEA agents are guarding the plane at the airport. If all goes well, we'll be on our way back to Montana within the next couple of hours."

"If all goes well." She sighed. "I'm not holding my

breath. I don't feel like this is over. *El Chefe* doesn't give up that easily."

"We'll be ready." Rafe smoothed a hand down her arm. "We'll get you home."

"Home." She sighed. "Where is home? I can't go back to my apartment."

"Then make Montana your home. There are plenty of children who need someone like you to look out for their best interests."

She smiled up at him. "You make it sound so easy. My life was in Chicago."

"And is it still?" He kissed her forehead. "What's keeping you there?"

"What do I have in Montana?" she asked.

"Me and Lucy," he answered.

She cocked an eyebrow. "For how long?"

"As long as we both shall live?"

"Ah, put the poor guy out of his misery," the driver said.

Rafe laughed. "Briana, you might not have had the pleasure of meeting Bear and Swede. They work with Hank as some of his Brotherhood Protectors. Swede's prior Navy, and a SEAL. Bear was Delta Force, like me. And they're interrupting a private conversation."

"Problem is, you two lovebirds are making things too difficult," Bear said from the driver's seat.

"Bear's right," Swede said. "Admit you care for each other and get on with life."

Briana laughed. "We've only known each other for a week."

"A week…a month…" Bear shrugged. "You know what you know. I knew within the first couple of days I loved Mia."

"Same with me and Allie," Swede said. "In our line of work, we have to rely on our instincts…you know…gut feel. What is your gut telling you?" Swede turned and pinned Briana with his gaze.

Heat rose up her neck. "I've never been happier than the week we spent in the cabin in the mountains. But that doesn't mean Rafe feels the same."

Rafe pulled her into his arms, the hard bulletproof vest digging into her. "Oh, sweetheart, I do."

"There you go. End of discussion," Bear said.

"Not really," Swede argued. "It's only the beginning."

"The beginning," Briana sighed. "I like the sound of that."

# CHAPTER 13

RAFE HELD Briana in his arms the entire trip back to Montana. He felt that if he let go, she'd slip through his fingers and be gone again. He wasn't ready to let her go and hoped she'd stay with him in Montana.

The big question was *as what?*

Was a week together enough to know if you were right for each other? Did he want a commitment from her? Did he want to marry her? Maybe the question he should've been asking himself all along was whether he was willing to lose her.

After her abduction, he knew the answer to that question.

*No.*

When they arrived at the airport in Bozeman, Hank called Sadie, waking her up, to let him know he was on the ground and would be home in less than an hour. The other guys all called their ladies and let them know they'd be home soon as well. The atmosphere was jovial, if not completely happy. They'd extracted both women and none of their people had been killed or injured badly.

The big downer was that *El Chefe* had gotten away.

Alejandra and Briana rode in the SUV with Hank and Rafe. Swede, Taz, Bear, Boomer and Chuck rode in the other. Rather than go to Hank's ranch, where they'd all parked their own vehicles before they'd loaded up weapons, communications and personnel for the trip to El Salvador, Chuck would drop them off at their homes so they could get some sleep.

In the early hours of the morning, Hank drove up to the ranch house. The lights were all out.

"That's unusual," Hank said as he shifted the SUV into park. "Sadie always leaves a light on the porch and one in the living room when I'm away."

"Maybe she forgot," Rafe suggested.

"Maybe," Hank said, a frown settling between his eyebrows. "Leave the gear in the vehicle. We can unload it all tomorrow. Everyone will want to get sleep. And speaking of home…Donovan and Briana, you two can stay here for the night. It might be safer than the cabin. Alejandra, you'll stay with us until we can figure out something. Right now, we all need sleep." He pushed open his door and stepped down.

Rafe got out and held the door for the two women. He'd stripped out of his bulletproof vest but wore a shoulder holster with his Glock. With *El Chefe* loose, he could have his mercenaries make another attempt on Alejandra or Briana. He'd had enough time to make some calls while they were in the air.

Hank led the way up the stairs to the porch, shaking his head. "It's not like Sadie to leave the lights off. At the very least, I would've thought Maddog would've left one on. He was in charge of ranch security while we've been gone." When he reached for the door handle, it turned without resistance. Hank held up a hand with his fist clenched, the sign for his team to stop. He pulled his weapon from the holster beneath his jacket, stood to the side of the door and nudged it open.

"Both of you get behind the SUV," Rafe said to Briana and Alejandra. He pulled his weapon from his holster and climbed the porch steps, moving to the opposite side of the front door.

Hank nudged the door wider and dove in, rolling to one side and to his feet in a hunched position behind a table in the foyer.

Rafe dove in as well and remained in a prone position on the floor.

A light blinked on, illuminating the living room.

Hank cursed.

Sadie sat in a straight-back wooden chair, her arms secured behind her, duct tape across her mouth.

In a playpen beside her lay her little girl, Emma, sound asleep.

Sitting in a wing-back chair beside them was *El Chefe*, holding Alejandra's baby, Bella, in his arms, a gun pointed at her little head.

Two of his men stood behind him, AK-47s in their hands, pointed at Hank and Rafe.

"It took you long enough to get here after you destroyed my home," the cartel leader said. "I don't forgive transgressions easily." He shrugged. "Actually, I don't forgive transgressions at all." The man glanced down at the baby in his arms. "I get what I want. Every. Time." He glanced toward the door. "Is that not correct, Alejandra?"

Alejandra entered through the front door, her eyes rounded and shaking her head. "I'll go with you. Just don't hurt her. She's innocent. She's your daughter."

"I thought as much. Another reason for her to return to El Salvador with her mother." He brushed the baby's hair back with the barrel of the gun he held. "It would a shame for her to die for no reason but that you didn't care enough about her to stay where you belong."

Alejandra looked from *El Chefe* to Sadie, Hank and Rafe. "Leave these people alone, and Bella and I will go with you. Now. This minute. No argument."

"You'll go with me no matter what I do with the rest of your friends."

"Please, they only wanted to help me," Alejandra begged.

"As I told your beautiful friend, Briana, I didn't get where I am by being kind to strangers. I take my business seriously. When people interfere in my business, they pay." He pushed to his feet.

The baby whimpered.

"Let me hold her." Alejandra walked forward, her arms out. "She's probably hungry and hears my voice."

As if to prove her mother right, Bella's whimpers turned into soft cries. She stretched and raised her arms, as if seeking Alejandra.

The cartel leader quickly became impatient with the baby and struggled to hold onto her and his gun at the same time. He almost dropped her.

Alejandra rushed forward to catch Bella.

*El Chefe* let her have the child and grabbed her instead, shoving his gun up against her temple. "Now, we are going to walk out of here, and none of you will stop us. If you do, I will kill the woman and the baby." He held out his hands. "The keys to your vehicle."

Hank dug in his pocket and pulled out the key fob, tossing it at the cartel leader. The fob landed at his feet.

"Get it," he told Alejandra.

Balancing Bella in her arms, Alejandra bent to retrieve the key fob.

*El Chefe* held the gun to the back of her head the entire time until she handed it to him. He pocketed the key fob and hooked his arm around Alejandra's neck, again pointing the gun at her temple.

With the keys to the SUV, the man was about to walk out of the ranch house with exactly what he'd come for. Alejandra and her baby.

Rafe's heart skittered to a stop and then raced. He prayed Briana had headed for the woods to hide until the cartel leader and his men were gone. The farther away she was, the better. Especially if *El Chefe* was taking the SUV she was supposed to be hiding behind.

*El Chefe* backed toward the door, holding Alejandra in a chokehold. His men followed, also backing toward the door, their AK-47s pointed at Rafe and Hank.

"If they move, shoot the woman," *El Chefe* said. Then he backed through the door and out onto the porch.

A loud crack rang out in the darkness.

The cartel gunmen turned toward the sound.

At that moment, Rafe sprang at the man nearest him, grabbed his rifle and shoved it up in the air.

Hank went for the one on his side and did the same.

Rafe's guy pulled the trigger, shooting a hole in the ceiling. They struggled for control of the weapon. Fueled by searing anger and pure determination, Rafe slammed the weapon into the man's face. It hit the guy's nose with a sickening crunch. Blood gushed from his nose, and his eyes teared. His grip weakened on the gun.

Rafe seized control and slammed the butt up hard, catching the man in the chin. He fell backward, hitting his head against wall. He slid down, knocked out cold. Rafe flipped him over, yanked the cord from the nearby curtains and tied the man's wrists together behind his back and leaped to his feet.

Hank had the other man on the ground, the AK-47 pressed against his throat.

The man's face was turning purple as he choked off his air supply.

Rafe ran for the door. He had to stop *El Chefe* before he got away with Alejandra and her baby. And he had to find Briana.

With his gun in his hand, Rafe stepped through the door. What he saw made his heart leap into his throat.

Alejandra stood on the ground below the porch, holding her baby close to her chest. "Please, don't hurt her."

The Devil Boss stood nearby with his hand twisted in Briana's hair, a knife pressed to her throat, blood trickling from a gash on the side of his head. "Bitch," he said through clenched teeth, swaying slightly. "I should have killed you in El Salvador. *Eres un problema.*"

Alejandra spoke in rapid Spanish, her voice passionate, desperate. Then in English, she said, "Kill her, and I will expose all of your clients, in every country."

"If you do not come with me, I will kill her." He lifted his chin and winced. "Who will win this argument?"

Briana captured Rafe's gaze and mouthed the words, *Shoot him.* Then she slammed her head backward, hitting *El Chefe* in the nose. The arm holding the knife shook.

Before he could tighten his hold, Briana cocked her arm and jammed her elbow into his side then ducked.

Rafe aimed and shot the cartel leader in the chest.

*El Chefe's* eyes rounded. The knife fell from his hand, and he clutched his chest. "*Debería haberte matado.*" He fell to the ground and lay still.

Alejandra walked over to the man and pushed his face with her foot. "But you didn't kill her." She spit on him and turned away, holding Bella close. "And I am thankful for the woman who was kind to this stranger." She hugged Briana and let the tears fall.

Hank ran out on the porch, breathing hard, a bruise turning purple on his cheek. "Is he dead?"

Rafe descended the steps, holding his gun out in front of him. He nudged the cartel leader with his foot then bent to feel for a pulse at the base of his throat.

"He's dead," Rafe said and stood. He went to Briana and pulled her into his arms.

Hank ran back into the house. Moments later, he emerged with his wife and daughter. "Sadie said Maddog went out to the barn to check on the horses because they were making a lot of noise. He didn't come back." He handed Emma to Sadie. "I'm going to check on him."

"I'll go with you." He handed his gun to Briana. "You know how to use it."

She nodded. "Be careful."

Rafe followed Hank out to the barn behind the house. As they approached, they could hear the muffled sound of someone yelling and pounding on the wall inside. The barn door had been wedged shut with a two-by-four board jammed into the dirt.

Rafe kicked it out of the way and flung open the door. The yelling grew louder.

"He's in the tack room." Hank flipped a switch on the wall. Nothing happened. "They cut the power to the barn." He turned and grabbed a flashlight from a hook on the wall and pressed the button, sending a beam of light through the building.

The horses in the stalls stirred, whinnying at the disturbance.

Hank hurried to a door on the right side of the barn. Another board had been jammed into the ground, bracing the door to keep it from opening. He kicked it aside, and the door burst open.

A big man with black hair and dark eyes charged

through, blood on his hands and shirt. He grabbed Hank by the front of his shirt. "Sadie?"

"Is fine. As is Emma."

"They hit me from behind. I fought them, but they won and threw me into the tack room. When I came to, I couldn't get out."

"At least they didn't just shoot you."

"They didn't bring silencers. Maybe they didn't want to wake Sadie," Rafe said.

"You're alive. My family is safe. That's what's important," Hank said. "Their leader is dead, and the two goons he brought with him are tied up in the living room."

Maddog shook his head and winced, rubbing the back of his head. "I shouldn't have let Kujo take Lucy to his place for the night. She would've warned me."

Rafe nodded. "I was about to ask. I'm glad to know she's okay."

"Come on, let's get back to the house. It's been a long night, and you might need medical attention," Hank said.

"I'm fine. Just pissed that they got the jump on me."

Rafe led the way back to the house, eager to get to Briana. He didn't like her being out of his sight. Not with all that had happened.

She was inside the house with Sadie and Alejandra, standing guard over the two cartel men.

"I called the sheriff and Homeland Security,"

Briana said. "They're on their way, along with an ambulance to collect this scum." She nodded toward the two men she had her weapon pointed at. "You want your gun back?" she asked Rafe.

He grinned. "Not unless you're tired of holding it. You're amazing."

She shook her head. "I'm not amazing. I'm shaking."

Rafe crossed the floor and took the gun from her trembling hands. "I've got it. You might want to sit before you fall."

"I'd rather stand here with you," she said and wrapped her arms around his waist.

He pulled her close with his free hand and kissed the top of her head. "I've been thinking about it. I really want you to stay in Montana."

She laughed. "Why? It doesn't appear to be any safer than Chicago."

"Maybe not, but I want you to stay with me. Like Bear and Swede said...go with your gut. Mine is telling me you're the one." He frowned down at her. "Unless your gut isn't saying the same thing."

Her arms tightened around him. "My gut is saying the same."

"If you really want to go back to Chicago, I'm sure I can find something to do there," he offered. "But Lucy wouldn't be nearly as happy as she is here in Montana."

Briana smiled up at him. "We do need to consider

what would make Lucy happiest. She's ours now."

"And we can't break up a family, can we?" Rafe said, bending to claim her lips.

"Why don't I take that gun for now," Hank drawled.

"I believe I see headlights coming this way," Sadie said. "And the sun's starting to rise. Emma will be awake in an hour or two. I'm going to take her to her room and tuck her in." She turned to Alejandra. "I'll show you to the room Bella's been sleeping in. It has a bed you can sleep in. You can nurse her there. Poor Bella hasn't been too happy with the formula."

Alejandra turned to Hank.

He nodded. "Go with Sadie, for now. I'm sure the police and Homeland Security will want to speak with you before you call it a night...or day, in this case."

"I'll be out as soon as I've fed Bella." Alejandra and Bella followed Sadie and Emma out of the living room.

Two sheriff's vehicles arrived with an ambulance following close behind.

Homeland security arrived an hour later.

The sun had fully risen by the time authorities left with the two cartel men and the body of *El Chefe Diablo.*

Emma woke. Sadie and Hank moved to the living room where Emma could play while Hank napped on the couch.

Sadie showed Briana to a room down the hall from Alejandra. She frowned. "Do you two need separate rooms, or just one?"

"One," Rafe and Briana said at the same time

Sadie laughed. "I kinda thought so, based on all the canoodling you've been doing since you got back. Besides, the Crazy Mountains have a way of bringing people together. You must be exhausted. I'll bring you some night clothes, and this suite has its own bathroom, so you don't have to leave it."

"Thank you, Sadie," Briana said. "Seems like I'm always borrowing clothes from you. I'll be glad when I can retrieve my own things."

Sadie's face brightened. "So, you'll be staying in Montana?"

Briana looked up into Rafe's eyes. "Looks that way."

His heart bursting, Rafe grabbed Briana up in his arms, kissed her soundly then pushed through the door into their suite. They didn't come out for a full day, thanks to Sadie leaving trays of food and piles of clothes outside the door.

Rafe would've stayed locked in the room forever. He knew without a doubt Briana was the one for him. When they finally had to come out and be social, he'd do something to make it more permanent. But for now, he was happy to make love and sleep with the woman he loved. Tomorrow would get there all too soon.

# EPILOGUE

"Briana, will you grab that other tray of steaks and bring it out to the porch?" Sadie called out as she left the kitchen with a bowl full of corn on the cob drenched in butter and wrapped in foil, ready to go on the grill.

"Got it," Briana said. "Are the baked potatoes nearly done?"

"Hank swears they'll be ready in five more minutes," Alejandra said. "And a good thing. Five trucks just pulled up."

"I hope we have enough food." Sadie turned to back out of the front door onto the porch. "I didn't really think the Deltas would actually come all the way from Fort Hood, Texas, for our 4th of July celebration."

"Are you kidding?" Rafe held the door for her. "They would've come even without the invitation.

I've been telling them about the fly fishing and rafting and wildlife they're missing out on. They all decided to pack up and come for a long weekend. Briana and I have got them all lined up for some Crazy Mountain fun."

"Where are you going to put them?" Sadie asked as she handed the bowl of corn cobs to Hank at the giant grill.

"We arranged for them to stay at the bed and breakfast in Eagle Rock," Briana said. "They'll like that, since they can walk over to the Blue Moon Tavern for dinner and drinks after a full day of hiking, fishing or rafting."

"Oh, good," Hank said. "Here they are now. Looks like my team is bringing up the rear."

"I think you could use a parking lot guide." Briana laughed. "Look at the caravan of vehicles heading this way."

The Delta Force team parked, grabbed beers and found chairs on the lawn.

"You weren't kidding about this place being amazing," Rucker Sloan lifted a beer to Rafe. "Glad you talked us all into coming up. Nearly gave the CO a coronary when we all asked off at the same time. If anything happens and we need to deploy, we'll do it from here."

"Man, I'm looking forward to the fly fishing," Bull said. "But right now, I'm looking forward to that steak Hank's got grilling."

Blade leaned back in his chair and stared out at the setting sun. "What's the nightlife like around here? Any lonely females in the neighborhood?"

"Can't you go an entire weekend without sniffing out a girl?" Mac clapped a hand on Blade's shoulder. "Problem is, you haven't found the right one. Not like our team jumper, Donovan." He tipped his head toward Rafe. "You look too stinkin' happy, man. You'll have us all convinced we need to get hitched by the time we leave Montana."

"What are you talking about?" Dawg frowned. "Did you get hitched, Donovan? When were you going to tell us?"

"Keep your britches on," Tank said as he climbed the porch steps and shook Rafe's hand. "They aren't hitched, yet." He smiled at Briana. "Make him do it right. Down on his knee and everything."

Briana grinned and looked at Rafe. "You might need some tips from Tank." She narrowed her eyes at the man. "You know so much, why haven't you gotten down on one knee yet?"

He shook his head. "Too stuck in my ways. No woman would have me."

"You're wrong," Briana said. "I'm sure the right one is out there, waiting for you to find her."

Joseph Kuntz arrived with his woman Molly Greenbrier and their dog, Six. "Did you start the party without us?"

"Hey, Kujo," Hank called out. "We were waiting

for you." He slapped a beer in Kujo's hand and turned to Molly. "Beer, wine or a margarita?"

"I'll have a beer," she said.

Kujo twisted the top off the beer and handed it to Molly.

Six found Lucy lounging in the shade on the porch and laid down beside her.

Boomer and Daphne arrived with Maya. They spread a blanket on the ground beside the one where Emma was playing with a plastic horse.

"Won't be long before Maya is chasing Emma around the barnyard," Sadie said.

"I can't wait to teach them how to ride horses," Daphne said.

"How are your riding lessons coming along?" Hank asked.

Daphne grinned. "Good. Boomer's going to get me a horse as soon as we build a barn on our place."

Hank grinned. "Then you'll need to get a pony for Maya."

"We will, when she gets a little bigger," Boomer said.

Taz Davila and his woman, Hannah Kendricks, the physical therapist at the local veterans rehabilitation ranch, arrived at the same time as John Wayne Morris—the Duke—and Angel Carson, his stunt-woman fiancée. They claimed the horseshoes and started a game far enough away from the little ones to keep them safe.

Swede and Allie had come earlier to help with setting up tables and making side dishes for the growing crowd of people.

Bear and Mia Chastain arrived with Chuck, Kate and Kate's niece Lyla.

Maddog and his woman Jolie pulled in shortly after.

Bringing up the rear were Viper and his woman, Dallas.

"Is that all of us?" Hank asked.

"Flannigan is out on assignment," Sadie reminded him.

"That's right." Hank dropped a foil-covered corn cob on the grill.

Sadie smiled and rubbed her growing baby bump. "Hank's really built quite the empire of protectors. I might decide to give up acting to help him keep organized. That and be a fulltime mom."

Hank handed the grill duties over to Swede and came up onto the porch to hug his wife. "You can do whatever your heart desires." He kissed her soundly and bent to kiss her belly. "Us guys will keep you busy here on the ranch."

"We don't know if the baby is a boy or a girl. We said we'd wait and be surprised." Sadie frowned. "You didn't peek at the ultrasound, did you?"

Hank grinned and waggled his eyebrows. "If I did, I'm not telling."

"Hank!" Sadie swatted at his arm.

Rafe slipped up behind Briana and covered her belly with his hands. "I can't wait for you to be as big as Sadie."

Briana leaned back in his arms and smiled. She'd meant to wait and tell him later that night when they were in bed at the hunting cabin, but now was as good a time as any. "Careful what you wish for, babe." She turned in his arms. "In eight and a half months. I'll be just as big."

Rafe's brow dipped in a frown. "Wait...what?" His frown deepened. "Are you saying what I think you're saying?"

She nodded, her smile spreading across her face. "I'm pregnant."

"What?" Sadie's head came up. "Briana? You're pregnant?"

Briana's grin broadened. "I am."

Dash Hayes glared at Rafe. "What the hell, Donovan?"

"Well, damn," Rafe muttered. "I was going to save this for a private moment, but since you're making announcements, I'd better make one of my own and also make an honest woman out of you." Rafe dropped to one knee. "Am I doing it right, Tank?"

Tank rolled his eyes. "If you have to ask, you aren't."

Briana's heart fluttered and swelled to twice its size, filling her chest with all the happiness she felt.

"Briana Hayes…" Rafe paused. "Hell, I had it all memorized, and now I can't remember a word."

"From the heart," Tank prompted. "Speak from the heart."

"Oh, right." Rafe cleared his throat and started over. He took her hand in his.

Briana's entire body trembled. She thought she might pass out or throw up, she was so nervous.

"From the heart," Rafe said. "From the moment I heard your voice talking to me from Chicago to Springfield, I felt like I'd come home. You have the most beautiful voice. Sometimes, I close my eyes and just listen to you talk. But I digress. The point is, I want your voice to be the one I wake to every morning. You're beautiful, courageous and fun to be with. Will you be my wife and make me the happiest man on earth?"

Briana cupped his cheeks in her palms. "Rafe Donovan…I thought you'd never ask." She laughed. "Yes! I've loved you since we met over the phone, and I'll love you when we're old and gray. And I can't think of anyone I'd rather have as the father of my child."

"Our child," he corrected. "And, oh yeah." He rose to his feet, dug in his pocket and pulled out a ring with a fat diamond solitaire surrounded by a halo of smaller diamonds. "Guess I should have started with this." He slipped the ring on her finger. "I love you,

Briana. Now, tell your brother not to kill me. Unless he wants to raise his nephew."

"Niece," Briana corrected.

Rafe frowned down at her. "Did you peek at the ultrasound?"

"If I did," she grinned. "I'm not telling."

"Well, we'll just have to wait and see who's right."

"Donovan, you've got a lot to learn," Hank said. "The woman is always right."

Rafe nodded. "And she's right. The right one for me."

"And it's too early to tell the sex anyway," Hank added.

Sadie clapped her hands. "Well, yay! We're going to have a wedding. And we'd better make it before the baby's born. Double congrats!"

Rafe pulled Briana into his arms. "Do you have any idea how happy you make me?"

Briana brushed her lips across his. "If it's anywhere near as happy as you make me, I might have a clue."

## THE END

Thank you for reading Delta Force Rescue. The Brotherhood Protectors Series continues with Dog Days of Christmas. Keep reading for the 1st Chapter.

. . .

Interested in more military romance stories? Subscribe to my newsletter and receive the Military Heroes Box Set

https://dl.bookfunnel.com/tug00n7mgd

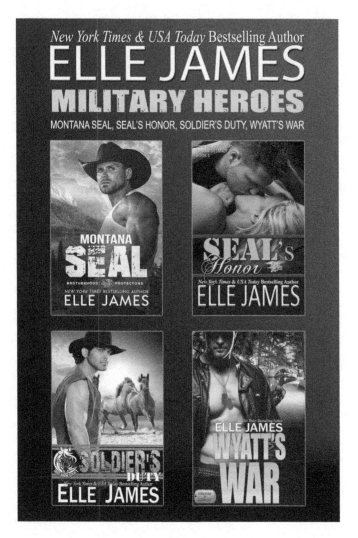

Visit ellejames.com for more titles and release dates
For hot cowboys, visit her alter ego Myla Jackson at
mylajackson.com
and join Elle James and Myla Jackson's Newsletter at
http://ellejames.com/ElleContact.htm

# DOG DAYS OF CHRISTMAS

## BROTHERHOOD PROTECTORS BOOK #16

*New York Times & USA Today*
Bestselling Author

**ELLE JAMES**

# DOG DAYS OF CHRISTMAS

BROTHERHOOD PROTECTORS

*NEW YORK TIMES* BESTSELLING AUTHOR

# ELLE JAMES

# CHAPTER 1

MOLLY GREENBRIAR STOOD at the window in the maternity ward at the Bozeman hospital, staring at the baby lying in the bassinet and sighed. "He's beautiful."

Joseph "Kujo" Kuntz grunted. "Kind of red and wrinkly, if you ask me."

Molly elbowed Kujo in the belly. "That's not nice," she said. "Babies are a miracle and should be treated with respect. That little human came out of Sadie's body."

Kujo shook his head. "That, in itself, is kind of scary." He jerked a finger in the nursery's direction. "Look how big that baby is. It's hard to believe he came out of his mother. Sadie's not a big woman. She's got a small frame. How did she push that kid out?"

Molly laughed. "A woman's body is built to adjust

to allow the baby to pass through. I'm sure it hurts like hell, but the result is well worth it."

Kujo's forehead creased. "Are you sure you want to have a baby? That's almost like asking for pain. Like me asking for someone to shoot me in the gut."

She gave him a twisted smile. "Not helping, Joseph. Not helping." She looked at the little boy swaddled in the hospital receiving blanket, wearing a blue knit beanie. The card tucked into the slot in his bassinet read "Baby Boy Patterson."

Molly sighed again. "What if we can't get pregnant?" she asked. "Have you thought about that?"

Kujo shrugged. "We have Six. He's turning into nothing but a big ol' baby."

She smiled. "He is a big baby of a German Shepherd, isn't he? But he's getting old. He's not going to be around forever. We've got three, maybe four more years with Six."

Kujo's frown deepened. "That dog's going to last forever. He's got nine lives, like a cat. He'll probably outlast all of us."

Molly shook her head. "On average, German Shepherds live to be between nine and thirteen years old. Fourteen, if they're lucky and stay healthy throughout their lives. Six is nine now, and he was wounded in the war."

"But he's getting the best treatment now," Kujo argued.

"Yes, but that won't help him to outlive us." Her brow wrinkled. "Don't you want children?"

Kujo slipped his arm around Molly. "You know I do. But if we don't have kids, I have you. You're all I really need."

She leaned into him. "Even with my career in the FBI, somewhere down the line, I've always imagined having a home, a husband and two-point-five children like everyone else in the country." She smiled wistfully. "When I married you, I imagined having a little girl with black hair and ice blue eyes."

He shook his head. "No, she'd look like you, with your red hair and green eyes. A little spitfire, just like her mama."

"Or a strapping boy with your broad shoulders and brooding eyebrows. Someone you could toss a football with or teach how to train dogs. Couldn't you just see two little children playing with Six? We might even get a puppy for them to play with."

Kujo drew in a deep breath and let it out slowly. "We've been trying for six months. You'd think by now something would've taken."

"Yeah," Molly said, her gaze on Baby Patterson. "I had hoped that by the annual Brotherhood Protectors' Christmas Party at the Pattersons' house, I could announce that I was pregnant. Now, I'm pretty sure that isn't going to happen. I doubt seriously that we'll even have the Christmas party since Sadie's had her baby a couple weeks early. Hank's not going to want a bunch of people in his house with a new baby there and Sadie recovering from childbirth. Nor is Sadie going to feel like organizing and hosting a party. She'll be tired and up all hours, feeding and taking care of an infant."

"Again," Kujo said, "why is it you want to have a baby?"

She slapped his arm playfully. "You know why. I want to have your baby. I want us to be a family."

"We are a family."

"I know," she said. "Six is our fur baby. But I'd like a human baby, too."

Kujo cocked an eyebrow. "Even if it is wrinkly and red?"

"I promise you, when our baby comes, you'll be proud, even if it's purple and polka-dotted because it will be ours."

"Hey, you two," a voice said behind them.

Molly and Kujo turned to find Hank Patterson standing behind them with his three-year-old daughter, Emma, in his arms. Beside him was a tall, quiet cowboy Molly recognized as Sadie's brother, Fin McClain. He carried a huge bouquet of white roses, a balloon that said *Congratulations* and a teddy bear dressed in a pale blue shirt that read, *It's a Boy.*

Kujo held out his hand. "Congratulations, old man, on another successful mission and baby number two."

Hank shook the proffered hand and nodded. "I

always thought the physical demands on a body were pretty tough for Navy SEALs, but after seeing Sadie give birth to two children, I gotta say, BUD/S training pain ain't nothin' compared to giving birth."

Kujo turned to Molly. "See? You heard the boss. Why would a woman want to have a baby?"

Hank chuckled. "Beats the heck out of me. If men were the ones responsible for giving birth, it would be the end of the human race."

Molly shook her head. "You guys are too much. A woman's body is made for this. And our hormones fake us into thinking we want this—that there's nothing better in the world than holding your own baby in your arms." She glanced back at Baby Boy Patterson. "He's beautiful, Hank. Have you chosen a name?"

"Not yet," Hank said, staring at his son. "We're still thinking about it. Before he was born, we'd narrowed the list down to about five names."

"Which names did you like most?" Molly asked.

"I liked Krull the Warrior King, but Sadie nixed that. We came up with Chase, Ledger, Matt, Dakota and Tate." Hank grinned. "All I know is that he needs a strong name. He's going to have a big sister who beats up on him all the time. He needs to be a badass to handle that." Hank kissed his daughter's cherubic cheek. "Isn't that right, Emma?"

"Emma?" Molly raised an eyebrow. "She's one of

the sweetest baby girls a daddy could want." Molly touched the little girl's arm. "She's an angel."

"Yeah, but she's got three years on him now. That little boy is going to take all of her mama's attention for a while."

"You think she'll be jealous?" Molly asked.

"It's a distinct possibility," Hank said. "Hell, I'm a little jealous of the little guy. I barely get any of Sadie's attention now." He winked.

"You could name him Hank Jr.," Kujo said.

"I wouldn't wish that on any kid of mine," Hank said. "He deserves a name of his own, not to share mine."

Four other men and four women exited the elevator, laughing, and joined them in front of the nursery window.

"Good for Sadie for delivering a healthy baby boy three weeks early," Alex "Swede" Svenson said.

"How's she holding up?" Swede's girl, Allie, asked.

"She promised she'd make it through the holidays before she delivered," Swede said. "What happened?" He winked at Hank.

"He's my boy." Hank's chest puffed out. "Eager to get out of tight places and spread his wings."

"Guess that means the holiday party's off," Alex "Taz" Davila shook his head. "We were all looking forward to it."

His girl, Hannah, raised her hand. "Don't get us wrong. We just love getting together with rest of the

Brotherhood. With the party only seven days out, we wouldn't want Sadie to go to all that trouble after just having a baby."

Hank frowned. "I'll talk with her. Maybe we can have it at a location other than the ranch."

"We could all make it happen and take the burden off Sadie," Molly offered. "She does so much already. We'd love to pull it together for her."

"Again, let me speak with Sadie. Sadie loves Christmas. She plans so far ahead, she might have the entire party set, and I don't know about it." He grinned. "She's been humming Christmas tunes since Halloween and had the Christmas decorations up on Thanksgiving Day. That's how she rolls. A baby won't slow her down." He looked from Kujo to Molly. "When are you two going to have children of your own? I thought you were planning on having a kid soon."

Kujo's jaw tightened. "Some plans don't work out, no matter how much you try."

"Still not pregnant, huh?" Hank touched Molly's shoulder. "Sorry to hear that. I've heard of people who've tried and tried to have a baby. When they finally give up, it happens."

"I'm sure that will be how it happens for us," Kujo said.

"You're not giving up yet, are you?"

"Not yet," Molly said.

"We're still willing to keep trying the old-fashioned way," Kujo said. "The next step would be to have my little swimmers tested to see if I'm shooting blanks. And I'd rather have my fingernails pulled out than to produce a specimen in a cup."

"It could be me. My eggs might not be good," Molly said, wrinkling her nose. "We just don't know why it isn't happening."

"I'm sure it's only a matter of time." Hank shifted Emma on his arm. "Ready to go see Mommy?"

The nurse in the nursery had just changed Baby Patterson, returned him to his bassinet and rolled the cart to the door.

"That's our cue," Hank said. "We're going to see Sadie." He turned to Kujo and Molly. "You know if the stress is getting to you and it's keeping you from getting pregnant, you can always use the hunting cabin in the Crazy Mountains just to get away from the TV, internet and telephone. Sometimes, all you need is a place to go relax and get to know each other again. The key to the cabin is located underneath the flowerpot on the front porch. You're welcome to use it anytime. I'm sure Six would enjoy a romp in the snow up there, too."

Molly tilted her head, considering. "Is the cabin even accessible at this time of the year? It's been snowing up in the mountains."

"I've been up there after one of the major blizzards of the year. With the right truck, you can get there." Hank tipped his head toward Kujo. "Kujo's truck will make it up there. Anyway, it's a thought. Now, I've got to go see my beautiful wife who has given me two beautiful children. This will be the first time Emma gets to hold the baby."

Fin stepped ahead of Hank. "Let me go in before you and Emma. I want to congratulate my sister and give her these." He held up the bouquet. "I'll only be a moment."

"Sure." Hank gave Fin a head start, and then followed him down the hallway to Sadie's room.

Kujo and Molly didn't want to disturb Sadie, Hank and Emma's joyous bonding with Baby Boy Patterson. They left the hospital and drove away in Kujo's truck.

Molly turned to Kujo. "What do you think about Hank's offer?"

"What offer?" Kujo asked.

"Weren't you listening?" Molly shook her head. "He offered to let us use the hunting cabin in the mountains as a getaway. I have the next three weeks off for vacation from my job, and you don't have another assignment with the Brotherhood until the middle of January. Why don't we do it?"

He glanced her way. "Just going up to relax?"

She nodded.

"Not going to be monitoring your ovulation cycle?" he asked.

She shook her head. "Not once."

Kujo raised his eyebrows. "We're not going to

obsess over getting pregnant the entire time we're up there?"

Molly sighed. "No. I'm kind of tired of the whole process."

"Although I'm a stud," Kujo puffed out his chest, "sometimes, it's hard to perform on demand."

She laughed out loud. "Like it's ever hard for you to perform on demand."

"True," he said with a grin. "But it does take some of the fun out of it."

She laid her hand on his arm. "I'm sorry."

He shook his head. "Sweetheart, don't be. I want this baby as much as you do. But if it doesn't happen, I'll be all right. I'm just worried about you."

"Well, if we can't get pregnant," Molly smiled brightly, "we can always adopt more retired working military dogs like Six."

"He does seem a little bit restless lately," Kujo remarked.

"Did you notice that his limp has practically gone away?"

Kujo smiled. "Yes, I have, and I'm happy for him."

Molly glanced at him. "So, we're doing it?"

Kujo grinned. "Looks like we're going to the mountain cabin."

Smiling broadly, Molly clapped her hands. "Good. I'm looking forward to it." Maybe at the cabin, they could get some rest, and maybe get back some of their lusty mojo that had gone by the wayside with the push to make a baby.

When they arrived at their home, Kujo helped Molly down from the truck. She hurried inside to pack clothing and blankets for their stay in the cabin. She might be overpacking, but they needed enough supplies to stay a week in the mountains. In a basket, she packed sheets, down-filled comforters, towels and washcloths and a couple of candles for ambiance and light.

The cabin had no electricity or running water. For baths, they bathed in a nearby stream in the summer. In the winter, they'd have to heat water from melting snow. It would take a lot of time to heat enough water over the open fireplace to fill the large metal washtub. For the most part, spit baths would have to do.

Six greeted them at the door, tail wagging in a somewhat subdued manner.

"Is it me, or is Six depressed?" Molly asked.

"I don't know what's wrong with him," Kujo said. "But maybe we need to take him to a veterinarian before we go out to the mountain."

Molly tilted her head. "Or maybe the mountain is just what he needs. If he gets worse, we can bring him back down."

"He definitely hasn't been himself lately."

"Do you think he's lonely?" Molly asked.

"He used to be in a kennel with dozens of other military working dogs." His eyes narrowed.

Molly's brows knit. "Do you think he's missing other dogs?"

"He's been with me for over a year," Kujo said.

Molly's lips tightened. "And with me almost as long."

"We're his pack now."

"Well, I think he's sad."

He glanced sideways at her. "You think we need to get another dog to keep him company?"

Molly's lips turned up on the corners. "Is that what you'd like me to get you for Christmas? A playmate for Six?"

Kujo shook his head. "I'm not much into Christmas. If a playmate is what will make Six happy, I don't see a need to attach it to Christmas." He glanced at Molly. "Don't get me wrong. I want Six to be happy. But why wait until Christmas?" He went back inside and came out with a bag of dog food, Six's dog bed and several chew toys.

Molly smiled. "I feel like those couples with small children. They pack everything and the kitchen sink."

"For now, Six is our baby," Kujo said.

"And he'll always be," Molly said. "He means as much to me as he does to you." Maybe they didn't need a baby to be happy…

# ABOUT THE AUTHOR

ELLE JAMES also writing as MYLA JACKSON is a *New York Times* and *USA Today* Bestselling author of books including cowboys, intrigues and paranormal adventures that keep her readers on the edges of their seats. When she's not at her computer, she's traveling, snow skiing, boating, or riding her ATV, dreaming up new stories. Learn more about Elle James at www.ellejames.com

Website | Facebook | Twitter | GoodReads | Newsletter | BookBub | Amazon

Or visit her alter ego Myla Jackson at mylajackson.com
Website | Facebook | Twitter | Newsletter

*Follow Me!*
www.ellejames.com
ellejamesauthor@gmail.com

# ALSO BY ELLE JAMES

Shadow Assassin

### *Delta Force Strong*

Ivy's Delta (Delta Force 3 Crossover)

Breaking Silence (#1)

Breaking Rules (#2)

Breaking Away (#3)

Breaking Free (#4)

Breaking Hearts (#5)

Breaking Ties (#6)

Breaking Point (#7)

Breaking Dawn (#8)

Breaking Promises (#9)

### *Brotherhood Protectors Yellowstone*

Saving Kyla (#1)

Saving Chelsea (#2)

Saving Amanda (#3)

Saving Liliana (#4)

Saving Breely (#5)

Saving Savvie (#6)

Hot Zone (#3)

Hot Velocity (#4)

*Cajun Magic Mystery Series*

Voodoo on the Bayou (#1)

Voodoo for Two (#2)

Deja Voodoo (#3)

Cajun Magic Mysteries Books 1-3

*SEAL Of My Own*

Navy SEAL Survival

Navy SEAL Captive

Navy SEAL To Die For

Navy SEAL Six Pack

*Devil's Shroud Series*

Deadly Reckoning (#1)

Deadly Engagement (#2)

Deadly Liaisons (#3)

Deadly Allure (#4)

Deadly Obsession (#5)

Deadly Fall (#6)

*Covert Cowboys Inc Series*

Triggered (#1)

Taking Aim (#2)

Alaskan Fantasy

*Boys Behaving Badly Anthologies*

Rogues (#1)

Blue Collar (#2)

Pirates (#3)

Stranded (#4)

First Responder (#5)


Blown Away

Warrior's Conquest

Enslaved by the Viking Short Story

Conquests

Smokin' Hot Firemen

Protecting the Colton Bride

Protecting the Colton Bride & Colton's Cowboy Code

Heir to Murder

Secret Service Rescue

High Octane Heroes

Haunted

Engaged with the Boss

Cowboy Brigade

Time Raiders: The Whisper

Bundle of Trouble

Killer Body

Operation XOXO

An Unexpected Clue

Baby Bling

Under Suspicion, With Child

Texas-Size Secrets

Cowboy Sanctuary

Lakota Baby

Dakota Meltdown

Beneath the Texas Moon